D0114180

Stella Díaz
to the Rescue

Also by Angela Dominguez

Stella Díaz Has Something to Say

Stella Díaz Never Gives Up

Stella Díaz Dreams Big

STELLA DÍAZ to the RESCUE

¡Puedo ayudar!

ANGELA DOMINGUEZ

Roaring Brook Press
New York

Published by Roaring Brook Press
Roaring Brook Press is a division of Holtzbrinck Publishing
Holdings Limited Partnership
120 Broadway, New York, NY 10271 · mackids.com

Copyright © 2022 by Angela Dominguez.
All rights reserved.

Our books may be purchased in bulk for promotional, educational, or
business use. Please contact your local bookseller or the Macmillan Corporate
and Premium Sales Department at (800) 221-7945 ext. 5442 or by email at
MacmillanSpecialMarkets@macmillan.com.

Library of Congress Control Number: 2021916529

First edition, 2022

Book design by Trisha Previte

Printed in United States of America by LSC Communications,
Harrisonburg, Virginia

ISBN 978-1-250-76310-5 (hardcover)

1   3   5   7   9   10   8   6   4   2

Dedicated to my mom, my family, and Kyle

Chapter One

"Do you have the grapes?" I shout excitedly from the living room.

My big brother, Nick, joins in. "Yeah, Mom. It's almost midnight."

Mom pokes her head in from the kitchen.

"Si, niños. Un momento."

Our neighbor Izzy looks up from her phone. "Grapes?" She's here with her dad, Diego, to celebrate with us.

"Grapes are one of our New Year's traditions," I explain as I smooth out my sparkly sweater.

Izzy nods, but she still looks puzzled as Nick fills her in on our yearly grape tradition.

Mom says it started in Spain, but now people all over Latin America do it. Each person gets twelve grapes, representing the months of the year. You're supposed to make a wish with every grape you eat. However, Nick and I have never paid attention to that. We believe whoever finishes all twelve grapes first must be the luckiest. Unfortunately, Nick always wins. It's probably because I giggle too much at Nick to eat quickly. He looks like a chipmunk with his cheeks filled with grapes!

But I've been hoping that this year will be different. I have my game face on.

I love that New Year's Eve feels different from every other day of the year. It's the one night we get to stay awake past midnight and wear fancy clothes just to sit at home. More than anything, I love having the chance to start over and the opportunity to make the next year even better than the last. It feels magical!

It's also awfully nice to have friends with us for this New Year's. Even Biscuit, Linda's Chihuahua, is here, and he is wearing his nicest sweater. Linda is in the

Bahamas with her family, and we're dog sitting until she gets back tomorrow. I think having Biscuit here is a sign there might be a dog in my future.

"Look, the ball is dropping!" exclaims Izzy, pointing at the television. On the screen, the announcer is counting down in Times Square.

We count along from ten to one. Then at the stroke of midnight, Mom and Diego blow their party horns.

Nick and I race to eat our grapes as Izzy slowly nibbles on hers while texting her friends. Nick looks like he is going to beat me when suddenly he gets distracted by his phone buzzing. This is my chance to win! When I finish my last grape, I open my mouth and stick out my tongue.

"All done! It's official. I am the luckiest!"

Chapter Two

I sleep in later than usual the next morn-ing, and so does Biscuit. Not Mom, though. When I go downstairs to the kitchen, she's dressed in her exercise clothes and is busy setting up the blender. I watch as she tosses in some yogurt, milk, blueberries, and frozen spinach.

"*¡Buenos días! ¡Feliz año nuevo!*" she exclaims, wishing me a happy New Year.

Mom looks at the spice rack and grabs the cinnamon.

"It's time to eat well and start our resolutions."

Before winter break, we learned about resolutions

in Ms. Benedetto's class. They are basically goals people make for the year.

"And what are your resolutions this year, Mom?"

Mom turns on the blender and shouts over the motor's whirling noises.

"Focus on my wellness and get a promotion at work." She taps her chin. "Oh, and for us to become US citizens, of course."

I get all tingly inside when she says the word *citizens*. Mom is two days away from taking the big citizenship test. It's a hard test you take when you are trying to become a United States citizen. You have to know the answers to a hundred questions about US history, even if they ask only ten of them. I've been helping Mom by pretending we're on a quiz show and I'm the host asking her the questions. If Mom passes, then she, Nick, and I will finally become citizens and have a special ceremony.

"What about you, Stella? Do you have any resolutions?"

I nod. *So many*, I think. I grab my journal from my backpack to show her.

Besides getting a dog and becoming citizens, one of my resolutions is to have the Sea Musketeers pledge finally approved by our school district. Last fall, we prepared to do a big presentation for the city council so they would approve our pledge to cut back on plastic, but at the last minute, it was canceled! However, we finally

have luck on our side. We received our letter in the mail with the new date in March.

"Those are some good goals, *mi amor*!" Mom says, kissing my head. Then she grabs her thick green smoothie and pours herself a glass. "Yum, *que delicioso*!"

She fills up a second smaller glass and sticks a metal straw inside. "Do you want to try?"

I look at her eager expression. It's hard to say no to Mom, so I take a gulp.

Even though the smoothie is muddy green like seaweed, it's surprisingly tasty! I give her a thumbs-up.

Mom's cell phone buzzes and lights up. She leans over and takes a peek at the screen.

"Linda messaged. She's back home."

I stare down at Biscuit. "Time to go, my little friend."

We walk outside, and I ring Linda's doorbell. She must be excited to see him, because she opens the door right away.

"My two favorite creatures! Come on in!"

She motions us to follow her inside. She smells of coconut-scented sunscreen and has tan lines on her face from her glasses.

Linda picks up Biscuit. He covers her face with sloppy kisses.

"I missed you, too," she says, giggling. Then she turns to me. "How did my boy do?"

"He was perfect." I clasp my hands together. "Guess what! Mom says we might be able to get a dog this year, too."

"I'll put a good word in for you with her." Linda grabs something from her purse. "Now, this is for taking care of Biscuit," she says as she hands me a few bills.

Linda gives me some money whenever I take care of Biscuit, although I never keep it. It always goes directly into the Sea Musketeers club.

She continues, "And this is a little gift from my trip."

I squeal when she hands me a small cardboard box. When I open it, there is a little sea turtle carved out of white limestone resting on top of cotton balls.

"I saw it and immediately thought of you. The gal who sold it at the store also said it would bring good luck."

I give Linda a big hug.

"Thank you!"

Then I wave goodbye and head back home. As I squeeze the sea turtle in my hand, I think, *This is just what I need for my perfect year.*

Chapter Three

I wake up energized even though it is as dark as the abyssal zone outside. Winter makes the days shorter, and usually all I want to do is sleep in, but today is special. It's the first day back to school after three weeks, and more importantly, it's Mom's citizenship-test day. We all get up extra early, including Nick, to help Mom review during breakfast.

In between bites of my warm cinnamon-flavored oatmeal, I grab a couple of the homemade flash cards.

"Oh, here are two questions combined into one," I say, reading a card. "Who was the first president and the father of our country?"

Mom replies, "George Washington. *Eso es muy fácil.* Ask me a harder one."

Nick sips his chocolate milk and then asks, "How many amendments does the Constitution have?"

GEORGE WASHINGTON

Mom's eyes dart around, searching for the answer in her mind. She quickly remembers and shouts, "Twenty-seven."

Nick flashes her a thumbs-up. "Remember you only have to answer ten questions. Not all one hundred of them. It won't be that bad."

Mom shakes her head. "That's true, but I don't know which ten they will ask from the list. We better do some more."

Mom nibbles on her toast. She promises she'll celebrate with a full breakfast afterward. For now, it's only dry *pan tostado.*

While Nick asks her another question, I suddenly

have the worst thought. It's something I hadn't considered until this very moment. It might be the reason why Mom is so concerned about passing the test. I burst and say it aloud without thinking.

"Mom, if you fail the test, does that mean we have to move back to Mexico?"

While I love Mexico, I haven't lived there since I was two years old. That would be an ocean-size change, not to mention I'd have to leave the Sea Musketeers and all my friends.

Mom leans over to give me a kiss on the head.

"*No te preocupes*. It just means I'd have to take the test again, and I'd prefer not to do that."

I let out a huge sigh of relief and lean over the counter dramatically, which makes both Nick and Mom laugh.

Mom looks up at the clock. "It's time to go to school, *niño*."

"Don't worry, Mom. You're going to ace this test," says Nick as he stands up, grabbing his backpack.

We hear a car horn beep outside. Nick's best friend,

Jason, and his mom are here to drive Nick to school. As he walks toward the front door, he shouts, "Good luck, Mom."

"*Gracias, niñito.*"

After Nick leaves, I finish getting ready for school. Mom drops me off a little early so she can have extra time to get to the immigration office.

As I open the car door to get out, I look back at Mom. She is sitting still and staring ahead like she's concentrating really hard. I instantly recognize what she's feeling because I have felt it often. She is nervous! Seeing Mom anxious is probably the oddest thing I've ever seen in my life. Well, maybe the oddest thing outside of a picture of a fangtooth fish. It's a deep-ocean fish with a mighty underbite. Anyway, Mom is the bravest person I know in the world. She's the one who encourages me to try new things and to have courage. Still, we've been working toward our citizenship since we moved to the United States seven years ago. Now I'm almost nine and three-quarters. That's a long time!

I struggle to find the perfect thing to say to her, and then I remember my good-luck charm. I dig into my pencil bag.

"Do you want to borrow my sea turtle?" I ask. "Linda says it's lucky."

"No, that's okay, *mi Stellita*. A hug from you is all the luck I need."

"Then I'll squeeze you extra, *extra* hard."

Mom gets out of the car, and I throw both arms around her. I squeeze so hard that I even groan as I do it. That makes Mom belly laugh.

"That works. *¡Ahora tengo mucha suerte!*"

After I say goodbye, I head toward my school. Down the main hallway, I spy Mr. Don, our custodian, cleaning a water fountain. Even though I don't speak to him too often, I decide to be more outgoing and say hi. I take a deep breath and make sure to project my voice so he can hear me. That's a trick I learned in my old speech classes with Ms. Thompson.

"Good morning, Mr. Don."

He steps back, looking a little startled. I turn *roja* like my red sneakers. I must have projected too much.

"Hello, Stella!" His kind expression puts me at ease. "Did you have a good break?" Mr. Don is the best at remembering students' names.

"I did, and guess what!" I say, practically ready to burst.

He tosses a paper towel into a trash can and smiles. "What?"

"My mom, brother, and me might become citizens soon!"

He throws his arms up in the air. "Congrats! That's amazing, Stella."

I knew Mr. Don would be excited for me. He was born in the Philippines and became a citizen when I was in third grade. The whole school threw him a surprise assembly to celebrate. We even had cake! He looked so happy, with tears of joy in his eyes. I hope it's a life-changing experience for me, too. I'm about to ask him how it feels to be a citizen when the first bell rings.

"Uh-oh. You know what that sound means. Time to head off to class, missy."

I nod. "Have a good day, Mr. Don."

I walk into my classroom and see Anna, Isabel, and Jenny at my table. I run over to my seat and look around the room for Stanley. I make eye contact with

Ben Shaw, but he glances away. Although he doesn't pick on me anymore since Ms. Benedetto chatted with him about it, we don't exactly talk much. When the last bell rings, I scan the room one more time.

"Where's Stanley?" I whisper to Jenny. "He should be here. He was supposed to get back yesterday from Texas."

Jenny shrugs her shoulders. "I haven't seen him."

Not having Stanley in class is a little disappointing, but I can't focus on that, because Ms. Benedetto begins speaking. "Good morning, class. I trust you all had a great break."

Everyone chatters excitedly to each other. A few students even shout aloud what they did over the break.

"I went ice fishing," shouts Jeremy.

"I ate so many cookies," chimes in Isabel.

Ms. Benedetto holds her right arm in the air and raises her left hand to her mouth to signal to us to quiet down. "I thought we'd ease into our first day back with a video."

The class roars happily like a colony of sea lions.

As Ms. Benedetto finds the video online, Jenny says

softly to me, "You won't believe what I heard. My dance company is going to participate in a regional competition. I could win a ribbon and graduate to the next level at my school!"

"That's amazing," I whisper. "I can help. You can borrow my lucky sea turtle that Linda just gave me for the competition. You will definitely win."

"Yes, please!" she says, beaming.

While the video plays, I notice the good-citizenship bulletin board beside me. I should study it carefully since I'll be a citizen soon. At least I really hope so. I quietly read each of the star-shaped messages on the board. I see words like *honesty*, *kindness*, and *community*. The word repeated the most is *help*. It seems like helping others is the biggest part of being a good citizen. If I make this one of my resolutions, then it might send some *buena suerte* to Mom during her test. I'm determined to do whatever it takes. Because if Mom fails the test today, we'll remain aliens for longer.

In third grade, I discovered that since we're not citizens, we are called "aliens" by some. It means we were born somewhere else, but for a while, I kept imagining scary space aliens. Thankfully, Nick taught me that aliens are cool. For instance, many important people who contributed achievements to the United States, like Albert Einstein, were also aliens. While I almost like the word now, it doesn't quite have the same ring as *citizen*.

The clock moves as slow as a sea anemone, but as soon as it strikes three, I race out of the building with my lucky sea turtle in hand. Since Mom took a personal day from work, she should be out here. I search frantically for Mom and Nick until I find them standing by a wintry-looking tree. They both look serious.

"Oh no! You didn't pass!" I throw my arms dramatically into the air.

Nick starts chuckling.

Mom smiles. "I passed! And I got all ten questions right!"

I jump up and down. It's hard to stretch my arms up all the way with my parka on, but I try my best.

Mom says, "And can you believe I had to write a sentence down to prove that I can speak English?"

I stop jumping and roll my eyes. My mom has been speaking English since she was my age. She began taking classes in elementary school back in Mexico.

"When are we going to have our ceremony?" Nick asks.

"They said in about two months," Mom replies. "We'll get a letter in the mail with all the information soon."

I squeal. I wish it were tomorrow, but that is not too far away. Really, what's two months in what is going to be my best year ever?

"Well, what do we do now?" Nick says.

I reply, "I know. First, we get Oberweis ice cream."

"I hope they have the Berry American flavor!" Mom claps her hands.

Meanwhile, I tuck my lucky sea turtle back into my pencil bag. I know for sure it somehow helped my mom! My new resolution to become the most helpful citizen also must have been lucky. Now I just have to live up to my promise.

Chapter Four

Saturday morning, there are still leftover paper streamers and handmade confetti around the living room. We celebrated Mom's citizenship test like a second New Year's Eve. We even splurged on an Oberweis ice cream cake. It took us a while to agree on which flavor since they didn't have Berry American, but we settled on the birthday-cake one. It seemed the most celebratory. It had rainbow sprinkles, after all.

But this morning, the party vibe is gone. Everyone is too busy with their weekend activities. For instance, when I check on Mom, I see her speaking with my *tía* Juanis on the phone while stretching on her yoga mat at the same time. Looks like she is keeping her New Year's resolution to be healthier.

Then I spy on Nick, who is dressed in his karate uniform and practicing in his room for his tournament today. If he does well, he will earn his black belt. I lean through the doorway and observe him. Watching him expertly do his high kicks, I have no doubt he will pass.

Even Pancho, my betta fish, is busy swimming around his tank. After I feed him his pellets, I double-check my calendar, which Mom helped me create in the fall. It helps me keep organized. I grin when I see that it is almost time for my weekly Sea Musketeers meeting.

Our club has met almost every Saturday since it started last summer. But before my meeting, it's time for my weekly walk with Biscuit while Linda meets her friends for a book club.

On Biscuit's walk, I see Diego and Izzy coming down our street with yummy pastries in their hands. Izzy has split her time between her mom's and dad's places since her parents divorced. That was about three years ago, when she was ten. Whenever Izzy stays with Diego, they have their own Saturday activity where they go to the bodega nearby for breakfast treats. If I'm lucky, they bring me a pastry back. Thankfully, I have my sea turtle in my pocket, so I believe luck will be on my side.

"Busy day, Stella?" Diego asks, taking a bite of a *pastelito de guayaba*. That's a breakfast treat with a guava-paste filling.

I nod. I start listing all our activities on my free hand.

"Walk Biscuit, my Sea Musketeers meeting, Nick has his black belt competition, and probably some homework."

Diego whistles. "That Díaz family. You all are real go-getters."

I turn *roja*. I'm a little embarrassed, but mostly proud that he would call me that.

"Tell your brother I say good luck," says Izzy as she pets Biscuit on his side.

"I will," I reply.

I stare at their brown bag of treats. Sometimes I wish I had X-ray vision or, better yet, mind control.

Diego adds, "*¡Felicidades!* I hear your mom passed the citizenship test."

I smile. "She sure did!"

Mom must have texted him yesterday. Diego and Mom are friends just like Stanley and I are. Although I have to admit, I did flip out at first when I convinced myself that they might be dating. Nowadays, I wouldn't mind if they started dating. Diego is nice, and I'd definitely get more breakfast treats.

"Oh, and here's one for the road," Diego says, pulling out a mini *oreja* for me from the brown bag.

I lick my lips. *Oreja* is the word for "ear" in Spanish, but the name is where the similarities end. I don't know what other ears taste like, but this *oreja* is one sweet, flaky pastry. I chomp down on it immediately.

With crumbs still in my mouth, I say, "*¡Gracias! ¡Adiós!*"

Then I return Biscuit to Linda so I can head off to my family's busy day.

In the car, I sit in the back seat as Mom gets into the passenger seat and Nick drives. Nick finally earned his learner's permit, so he's allowed to drive the car on the weekend—but only with Mom's supervision.

When I get out of the car at Mariel's for our Sea Musketeers meeting, Nick calls from the front seat, "Wish me luck!"

"*¡Buena suerte!*" I reply, trying to kick in the air.

"*¡Pórtate bien!*" Mom jokingly tells me to behave. She knows that I rarely get into trouble. Then she gives me a kiss on the cheek from the passenger-side window.

Kristen and Logan arrive at the same time as I do. We fist-bump as we walk up to Mariel's door.

"I am so excited," Kristen whispers as she rings the doorbell.

Today's meeting should be especially great because

we are speaking with Mr. Kyle, our Shedd Aquarium summer-camp counselor, about the city council presentation. Not only did he help us create the original pledge during camp, but he also agreed to present as our special expert about the crisis with the oceans and plastics.

Mariel swings open the door.

"Follow me. We're going to hold the meeting in the dining room."

I see Mariel's parents getting the laptop ready for our virtual meeting. Stanley is already there, sitting at the table. It looks like he is wearing a new shirt covered in constellations. I beeline over to him and practically knock him over when I greet him.

"It's been more than three weeks!" I exclaim. "Why weren't you at school this week? And how are you?"

Stanley rubs his head. "Ugh. It's not been a good new year so far."

"Why?"

He leans forward. "We were stuck at the airport forever on our way back, and then I caught a stomach bug, and I was sick for a whole day. It was gross! Not to mention, I was also supposed to get a super cool tele-scope for Christmas, but it is lost in the mail!"

He rubs his hands over his eyes. "All of this makes me nervous that this will be a tough year."

I shake my head.

"That's impossible. It's going to be the best year ever."

His face pokes out from underneath his fingers. I can tell he doesn't quite believe me. I dig out the sea turtle from my pencil bag and place it on the table in front of him. His eyebrows furrow in confusion.

"Linda gave this to me, and apparently it's super lucky. You can hold on to it until Monday, and things will instantly improve for you. I promise."

He bends over and studies the sea turtle closely. "Stella, it doesn't seem particularly lucky, but I'll give it a shot."

I nod confidently. "You'll see." As I pull out the official club journal, I ask Stanley, "How was your winter break besides all the bad stuff?"

"Fun!" Stanley replies. "We drove to Galveston

and went to the beach for Christmas. We even visited Moody Gardens, where they have giant glass pyramids! How was your break?"

I tell him that my mom passed her citizenship test.

He gives me a high five. "So cool! That means you can be the president of the United States when you grow up."

I shake my head. "Only people who were born here can."

Logan chimes in. "You'll just have to settle for being the copresident of our club for now."

"Thanks, copresident," I reply, smiling at Logan.

Logan became the Sea Musketeers copresident last year. When fourth grade started, I became overwhelmed with all my new activities. While I fought the idea of having a copresident at first, since the Sea Musketeers was my idea, it's been really helpful to have someone to share the load with. Logan helps keep us on track, and he also has great ideas.

After Jenny arrives, we finally begin our video chat with Mr. Kyle. To set the mood, Mr. Kyle has a virtual ocean backdrop of a healthy coral reef on the screen.

Mr. Kyle starts. "What have you all been working on for the presentation?"

Stanley speaks up first, since he is holding the group's toy orca. Whoever holds it in their hands gets to speak.

"We were thinking you could share facts about Lake Michigan and how much litter is in there. And how that litter, especially plastic, eventually ends up in the ocean."

Mr. Kyle nods. "What's your name, young man? I don't recognize you from the summer camp."

"I'm Stanley."

Unlike the rest of the Sea Musketeers, Stanley and Jenny didn't attend the Shedd Aquarium summer camp with me. But when we formed the club, I knew they would want to join because they care about protecting the oceans, too.

Mr. Kyle replies, "Well, that's a great idea, Stanley."

Stanley grins widely. I point at my lucky sea turtle.

Stanley whispers, "Maybe you're right."

Logan takes the orca and says, "We also thought about mentioning how schools might be cleaner with less plastic waste." He pauses. "Is that a good idea?"

Mr. Kyle nods. "Definitely. I'll share with you some links I have found that show how other school districts have cut back. It saves them money, and it's a real win-win situation."

I glance over at my club members, and we exchange

excited looks. Then I write down all of Mr. Kyle's suggestions. One of my favorite jobs as copresident is recording all the notes in our journal.

After we finish our virtual visit, we brainstorm our next steps. I jot down a list of everything we need to do, like make a fun slideshow and posters that show the different steps in the pledge. Logan even suggests investigative photographs of messy trash cans at school.

At the end of the meeting, I make sure Stanley takes the lucky sea turtle home with him. I walk out of Mariel's house feeling like I'm on top of the world. With all our great ideas, there is no way that the council can turn down our proposal. Not to mention, it's only a few days into the year and I'm already being so helpful to my friends, like Stanley. Seeing him magically come up with a great idea, after I let him borrow the sea turtle, was the best.

My mood quickly changes when I walk up to Mom's car. Nick is in the back seat instead of the driver's seat. He looks uncomfortable.

I open the back door to get in.

"Nick, did you get your black belt?"

Then I look at Nick's foot. He has his right foot raised on his gym bag like it's injured. "What's wrong?" I ask.

He sighs. "I did get my black belt."

He points at his trophy lying on the car floor, then he groans. "But in the parking lot, I was goofing around with my friend and raised my trophy over my head. Then the trophy slipped out of my hands and landed on my foot *hard*."

I try not to giggle. The image in my head sounds funny, but he seems to be in a lot of pain.

Mom looks at me with a worried expression. "Stella, *por favor* get in, but carefully, next to your brother. We need to take him to the emergency clinic for an X-ray."

As we drive, my brother rests his foot on my lap. It looks pretty bruised, with a color like a fish called a purple tang. I try to pick up the trophy to take a look, but it's too heavy for me to lift. I glance back and forth from the trophy to his foot.

"I'm sure it's okay," I say, trying to be optimistic.

He nods. "Hopefully, or this is going to be a lousy year."

But something about the way he says it makes me unsure if it will be okay. If only I still had my lucky sea turtle in hand. Maybe none of this would have happened.

Chapter Five

A few hours later, we leave the emer-gency clinic with a cast that covers Nick's foot and ankle. Turns out that his foot is, in fact, broken. He will have to wear the cast for the next two months. Nick looks defeated as he hops back into the car.

"This completely ruins everything," he groans. "It's so embarrassing, too. What am I going to tell people? They are going to laugh at me when I explain how I broke it. Not to mention, how can I work at the pizza shop, drive the car, or do karate while I have this on my foot?"

Mom tries to comfort Nick. "You can keep the injury mysterious. That will make it sound more dramatic."

Nick shrugs. "I guess so."

Mom adds, "And I know it will be tough, but two months isn't that long. It's only one-sixth of the year."

"Yeah! Before you know it, you'll have your cast off and we'll be citizens, too," I say.

"Okay." But he doesn't sound convinced.

I remember one of my fun ocean facts and try to cheer him up. "At least you have bones. Some sea creatures like hagfish don't have many bones, and they aren't very attractive."

Nick doesn't reply. He silently rests his head against the car window and stays like that the whole way home.

When we get inside the house, we set up Nick on the couch. Mom grabs him the crutches from the hallway closet—the same crutches my *abuelo* uses when he visits—while I make sure to pick out the squishiest, softest pillows for him to elevate his foot. I also grab a blanket and place it on top of him.

"Thanks, sis," he mumbles.

Mom places a little bell on the coffee table. "Ring if you need anything, *niño*."

Nick doesn't respond. He's already fallen asleep on the couch.

"Must be the pain medication," Mom says, looking at him. She motions for me to follow her and whispers, "Let's watch television upstairs and let him sleep."

We watch an ocean documentary in Mom's room. We don't watch TV up in her room often, so this feels like a treat. Plus, Mom's bed is enormous and has more pillows than mine. It feels like resting on a giant marshmallow.

In the documentary, the camera follows a yellow pyramid butterfly fish. Amazingly, its head is naturally darker so it can seamlessly blend into low light environments. I make a mental note to write that down for a conversation starter. During a commercial break, Mom lowers the volume and leans over to me.

"You know, Stella, Nick is going to need our help for the next couple of months."

I nod. "I'll make sure to super-duper take care of him. I'll even make him those no-bake peanut butter cookies he likes. Anything he needs, I can help. In fact, it's one of my newest resolutions." I raise my hand to make it official. "I vow to be the most helpful citizen."

Mom chuckles. "My sweet *Stellita*. I knew I could rely on you."

Then she pauses. "Just remember to be patient with him, too. He may be grumpy at times. It's going to be frustrating for him to have to stay home and not do things the normal way for a while."

"Okay, Mom." But secretly, I know that is going to be impossible. With me helping him, I'll make sure that he's always happy. Any chocolate milk he wants, I can provide. If he needs a blanket or ice, I can assist. If he needs to hop somewhere and there are no crutches, he can lean on me. Then something big occurs to me.

"Wait, Mom. How am I going to get home from school every day if Nick can't walk me?"

Mom sighs. "*¡Ay caray!* I didn't even think about that! Let's make some phone calls and see."

"Don't forget about my art club, too! That's Tuesday and Thursday."

"*¡Claro que no!* We've got your schedule, after all."

I smile. Thank goodness Mom helped me make a schedule to stay organized.

While Mom makes phone calls, I check on Nick, who is still sleeping on the couch.

I whisper to him, "I promise to be the best nurse sister. That's what a good citizen would do." Then I tiptoe back to Mom's room.

After a few phone calls, we figure out my new after-school routine. Jenny's mom will give me a ride home most days, and Chris's mom will pick me up on art club days. I'm excited. Chris and I don't know each other that well yet, but we've started to become friends through art club. He knows so much about art and always manages to keep his paintbrushes clean. Mine always get gunky. I'm hoping if he becomes my good friend, he can share all his tips with me. I guess I'll find out this Tuesday.

My thoughts are interrupted by the sound of a bell ringing.

"That's Nick," I say to myself, and I run downstairs to help.

Chapter Six

I am so happy to be reunited with my lucky sea turtle again.

Stanley returns it to me before class on Monday. "You're right. It's so lucky! Not only did our Sea Musketeers meeting go well; my telescope magically appeared on our doorstep. It was delivered to the wrong house!"

I flash a grin and quickly grab the sea turtle from his hands.

"No more broken bones," I whisper to it, and then tuck it safely back into my pencil bag.

The next day, we have our first art club meeting of the new year. I'm particularly pumped about art club because at the end of last year, Ms. Benedetto and

Mr. Foster said that we were going to start a new project in January. I don't see how we can possibly top the mural we painted in the library. All I know is I've been drawing all winter break in preparation.

"Our last endeavor, the mural, was such a big hit," Mr. Foster says. "We thought we should do another big art event. Do you want to explain, Ms. Benedetto?"

"Of course."

She smiles at him and then glances down at her engagement ring.

Last year, I found out that Ms. Benedetto and Mr. Foster secretly *like* like each other. That secret didn't last long. Shortly afterward, they announced that they were engaged, and now everyone knows that they are a couple.

"Our big event is we're going to do a gallery show here at school," Ms. Benedetto says.

I clasp my hands together in excitement.

Mr. Foster adds, "It will be portraits of the faculty and staff at Arlington Heights Elementary. We'll have a big reveal during parent-teacher night in March."

Anna whispers, "I love drawing portraits."

I nod back. It's true! I've seen Anna's composition book, and the inside is covered in portraits of fairies.

Then Mr. Foster says, "And for some extra inspiration, we're going to visit the Art Institute. We applied for a grant and luckily, we received it. This means the field trip is all paid for, too."

I cover my mouth with my hand and softly squeal. The Art Institute is in downtown Chicago near the Shedd Aquarium. It's probably the loveliest art museum I have ever visited. Truthfully, I've never been to another one, but I've heard tourists say that, and I'd like to believe them. Mr. Foster hands out permission forms with dates, and my hands shake with excitement as I hold the paper. This school trip may be the inspiration I need to finally become a true artist.

"These portraits can be done in any style or technique," Ms. Benedetto says. "For example, you could use collage, paper cutouts, pencil, watercolor, and so on. All we want is for you to have fun with it."

I look over at Chris. I can tell he is as eager as I am to get started.

Mr. Foster adds, "Today, you're going to start on a series of self-portraits before the big portrait. This first one will be from your imagination. While you work, begin to brainstorm whose portrait you'd like to draw."

Chris leans in. "I don't need to brainstorm. I want to draw Ms. Bell."

I give him a thumbs-up. Ms. Bell was our third-grade teacher. I hope he draws her using pointillism since her favorite pattern to wear is polka dots.

Anna says, "I know who I'd like to draw, too! I want to draw Mr. Foster." She looks at me. "Whose portrait are you going to draw, Stella?"

I tap my finger on my head and think. Part of me wants to draw Ms. Benedetto, but I am sure everyone else will want to draw her. She's the coolest-looking teacher at the school. Someone probably should draw our new principal, but I've never been to Mrs. Hsu's office before. Then I remember my upcoming citizenship ceremony and Mr. Don. I could draw him! This is *perfecto*. I'll be able to spend time with Mr. Don, and on top of that, I can ask him all about what happens during the citizenship ceremony. Plus, this would be a good opportunity to recognize him for all his hard work to the whole school. This sounds like a project a good citizen should do. A citizen should make sure everyone gets their proper recognition.

"I think I'd like to do a portrait of Mr. Don."

Anna looks confused. "You don't want to draw one of the teachers?"

Chris pipes up. "I think that is a great idea. Mr. Don is awesome."

I smile at him as we continue on our imaginary self-portraits. I spend most of my time in art club drawing my many curls.

After the meeting, I walk with Chris to meet his mom. I feel a little nervous. It's my first time riding home with them. While we chat sometimes in school and at art club, Chris and I haven't spent time together outside of school. I follow him toward his mom's van. It has a customized license plate that reads VAN GO.

"It's an art joke," Chris says. "Like the artist Van Gogh."

I fake a giggle, but secretly I think I have to look up who this Van Gogh artist is.

Chris nods. "My family loves art. My mom is a graphic designer. She works from home."

"That is so cool!" I reply.

The side door on the van automatically opens, and Chris's mom greets us from the front seat.

"Hi, Stella. I'm Susan Pollard. I've met you before at a classroom party last year."

I wave. "Hi, Mrs. Pollard."

"You can call me Susan. Hop on in. We're happy to drive you home. Chris always talks about how talented you are at drawing."

I beam. I must be good at drawing if Chris says so.

When I jump into the back seat with Chris, I notice a sign with a wheelchair symbol hanging from the rear-view mirror. I stare at it, wondering what it means.

Chris must notice my staring, because he says, "We have that sign for my dad."

"Oh . . . ," I reply. I'm not quite sure what to say.

"He's in a wheelchair." He quietly looks at the floor. From his expression, I can tell he must feel very sad about his dad.

The look on his face quickly changes. "Mom, I think I see Summer's missing toy under your car seat."

"What a relief." She sighs. "I'll make sure to grab it when we get home."

"Who is Summer?" I ask Chris.

"My dad's dog." He tries to reach the toy with his feet. "She helps my dad get around."

His dad being in a wheelchair must be so hard for his whole family. I stare at Chris, thinking of something I could say to comfort him, and then I remember *mi abuelo*, Apolinar.

"My grandfather only has one leg," I say.

"Really?" He looks at me.

I nod. "It's tough. He uses an artificial leg and crutches sometimes."

Chris sympathetically smiles. "I'm sorry about your grandfather."

I reply, "I'm sorry about your dad."

It's silent for a moment, so I decide to change topics. "How do you think you're going to do Ms. Bell's portrait?"

He sits up proudly. "I'm not sure. I think I will

experiment with a few mediums until I figure out which is the best."

I'm so amazed he uses big, fancy art terms like *mediums*. It means the type of art materials an artist uses and not a clothing size.

"Chris, can I ask you something about art?"

"Sure!" he replies.

"How do you keep your paintbrushes so clean?"

He chuckles. "That's easy! You just need to use a big bucket of water to clean them off. That's something my grandmother taught me. She and I do those paint-by-number landscapes together. They are so fun."

For the rest of the ride home, we chat about our portraits and school. While I feel awful that Nick broke his foot, I'm sure glad I get to talk to Chris more.

Back at home, I am excited to finish my imaginary self-portrait. I am inspired by one of Frida Kahlo's famous self-portraits. Instead of a monkey and flowers like in Frida's painting, I decide to draw myself surrounded by my favorite things. I draw myself wearing a red beanie like Jacques Cousteau, with a dog and my

lucky sea turtle beside me. The last step is to color my skin in, but I can't find a colored pencil that matches my skin tone well. I decide to leave it blank.

When I go downstairs, I see Mom is preparing an easy dinner for us in the kitchen. It's vegetarian tacos *con arroz y frijoles*. Must be part of her wellness resolution.

She says, "*El arroz está listo*. Can you go check on your *hermano*?"

If the rice is ready, that means the rest of the dinner is done. I salute her. "Reporting for duty."

I check on Nick, who is sitting at the dining room table. He's talking on the phone and has his broken foot propped up on an empty seat. I wait until he puts his cell phone down.

"Who was that?" I ask.

"The pizzeria. They said I could take a break for the

next two months. I'll still have a job once my foot is all better and I can go back to work."

"That's great!" I say. I study Nick. He seems uncomfortable.

"Do you need a pillow?" I ask.

He stares at his cast, then at the hard chair his foot is resting on. He looks up at me.

"I guess so. I forgot to get one."

I grab a pillow from the laundry closet and place it gently under his foot. Then I walk to the kitchen and pour a small glass of chocolate milk for him.

"Whoa," he says when I bring it to him. "I could get used to this treatment."

I smile. "Mom says it's dinnertime."

He starts to stand up, but I stop him. "Don't worry. I'll bring that to you, too."

"Thanks!" Nick's chocolate milk mustache makes his grin appear even bigger.

I walk away feeling proud of myself. If there were a citizenship scorecard, I would have earned a check plus in the helpfulness category.

Mom calls from the kitchen. "¿Stella, *me puedes ayu-dar?*"

I reply, "Of course! I'm on my way!"

As I walk back to the kitchen, I whisper, "It's future citizen Stella Díaz to the rescue!

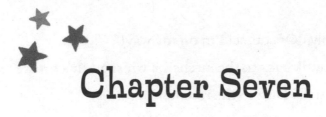

Chapter Seven

After school the following Friday, Stan-
ley, Jenny, and I decide to work on homework together
at my house. Ms. Benedetto assigned us a project on
waves for our science section. Since it's the three of

us together, we're allowed to walk from school to my home by ourselves.

"How has it been riding home with Chris?" Jenny asks, while stretching her hand out to catch a snowflake. There are only a few flurries. It's actually the first hint of snow that we have seen in a while. We haven't really had much since our big snowstorm in October.

"Fun." Then I stop. I don't know whether it's okay to ask, but I decide to go ahead and bring it up. "Did you know that his dad is in a wheelchair?"

Jenny shakes her head while Stanley nods.

"I went to a sleepover at Chris's house last year and met his dad. He's very nice and funny." Stanley pauses. "He has something called PLS, which is why he is in the wheelchair, but he didn't talk much about it."

I gulp. "Oh. I've never heard of that."

Stanley says, "We should look it up online when we take a break from homework."

"Good idea," I reply. "Which reminds me, I also need to look up information on Van Gogh."

When we get to my home, Nick is lying on the

couch in the living room working on homework. He has unofficially taken over the first floor since it's hard to go up and down the stairs with the cast on his foot. He looks exhausted as he reads a book for his English class.

Stanley looks at Nick's cast. "Whoa, does that hurt?"

Nick places his hands behind his head and leans back against a pillow.

"It's sort of a drag when I'm walking around school, but I manage okay. Even though it's broken in two spots, I still take the stairs sometimes instead of taking the elevator at school."

"You're really tough," Stanley replies, thoroughly impressed.

Nick looks proud, which is good, because I think he still feels embarrassed about how he broke his foot.

"Do you want us to sign your cast?" Jenny asks.

I jump up and down. "What a good idea! I hadn't even considered it."

Nick nods. "Okay, I guess so."

I run to grab some permanent markers from my room, and we begin to decorate his cast. I draw a smiling octopus with all eight legs while Stanley draws a rocket ship. Jenny writes her name in big bubble letters. She doesn't like to draw, but she's fabulous at lettering. She often draws letters for our Sea Musketeers posters. When we're done, we get started reading our handouts on waves at the dining room table. We have to stay close by to Nick because we're not allowed to be online without supervision.

From the little that I know, waves are simply amazing. They happen constantly and are usually generated by wind. Sometimes strong weather with high-powered winds, like tropical storms and hurricanes, creates huge waves. Tsunamis probably cause the biggest, most devastating waves. Those are caused by giant underwater earthquakes. While I love the ocean, learning about tsunamis makes me very glad that we live far away from them in Chicago.

Stanley reads aloud from our assignment sheet. "We need to write a paragraph each on two waves. The first paragraph should be on a big wave in history. The second should be about a big moment in our personal lives. Something that left a big impression."

We move to the laptop to begin our research. Jenny searches first. She exclaims, "Wow, did you know the biggest wave ever recorded was in 1958 in Alaska's Lituya Bay? It was one hundred feet tall!"

"That's like as tall as a building!" Stanley says. "We've got to include that."

I nod, but my mind is sort of distracted. Usually I would love to share ocean facts, but I keep wanting to know what exactly is wrong with Chris's dad.

I pull up another window in the browser and type in "PLS" in the search bar.

"That's not on the oceans," whispers Jenny. I shush her.

All our whispering must have been suspicious, because Nick shouts, "What are you guys working on?"

I turn a little *roja* and say in a high-pitched voice, "Waves . . ."

Nick looks over at us at the table from the couch. "And . . ."

I start sweating. The jig is up. I blurt out, "My friend's dad is in a wheelchair, and I want to learn more about his condition, so we were searching online. Only for a brief minute if not seconds."

Nick deepens his voice. "Stella, bring the computer over here."

We walk over to the couch with the laptop.

Nick sees what I typed in the search bar and scratches his head.

"I've never heard of this. Let me read first. This sort of stuff can be confusing."

"Can you look up Van Gogh, too?" I ask.

Nick motions at me to be quiet. "One thing at a time."

He looks at the website and reads quietly to himself. Then he frowns and puts the laptop aside.

"PLS stands for primary lateral sclerosis."

"What does that mean?" I ask.

Nick sighs. "I think we should wait for Mom to explain."

"Come on, tell us," I beg.

I can tell by his expression he doesn't want to say anything else, but I keep staring at him. Finally, he breaks down. "It's a very rare disease that makes you lose your ability to use your muscles well."

Stanley scratches his head. "I don't understand."

Nick explains. "It means their dad can't walk or move around as easily as most people, and it can impact his speech as well."

"Is there a way to make him better again?" I ask.

He shakes his head.

I gulp. I can't believe it. I've seen people in wheelchairs on the street, but I haven't known anyone who actually uses one until now. While *mi abuelo* might have an artificial leg, no one can really tell just by looking at him, and he still manages to do most things. And Nick might have to use crutches, but that's only for a couple of months. I can't imagine what I would do if I were in a permanent situation like Chris's dad.

"We've got to do something to help!" I exclaim.

Jenny and Stanley nod, but from their faces, I can tell they are as clueless as I am on what to do.

Nick looks at me with a sad expression. "Stella, some things can't be fixed as easily as a broken foot."

I cross my arms. That's impossible. There is a solution for everything. While I haven't read it in a good-citizenship manual, I'm positive a good citizen never gives up.

Stanley chimes in. "Stella, I'm sure we can do something to help, but we should get back to work on our homework. My dad is coming to pick me up in an hour."

The three of us do our homework silently. I try writing about a big wave in my life, but I can't focus on one idea now, not after learning what PLS means. My parents getting a divorce was rough, but it seems so small in comparison to a health condition. Most days, I don't even think about my parents not being together. I'm reminded only when I speak to Dad or when he behaves like not a great father.

I'm sure for Chris, his big personal wave was his dad getting sick. It seems awfully unfair that he and his family have to deal with that every day.

I pull my lucky sea turtle out of my pencil bag. I consider giving it to Chris, but I sort of need it until our citizenship ceremony just to make sure nothing goes wrong. I certainly don't want anything to disrupt that. All I know is this is a hard situation, and like a concerned citizen, I'm determined to help.

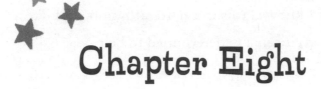

Chapter Eight

After Stanley and Jenny leave, Nick shows me a few paintings by Vincent van Gogh. They are unlike anything I've ever seen before. Nick reads from a web page that his paintings are Postimpressionist, meaning they are very colorful. His brushstrokes remind me of a whirlpool. We even find out that a few of Van Gogh's paintings are at the Art Institute. I can't wait to see them during our field trip, especially his self-portrait. It might be the perfect inspiration for my

VAN GOGH

portrait of Mr. Don. I hope I can make my painting look as amazing as Van Gogh's work.

I play around with my colored pencils trying to draw a parrotfish with swirly lines until Mom comes home. Parrotfish are fun to draw because their beaks are parrot-like. Mom walks in holding a letter she received in the mail.

"*Niños*, we've got our ceremony date."

"When?" Nick asks.

"Mark your calendars. It's March tenth!"

"Yay!" I reply. I can't believe how epic this March will be. Between the ceremony and the Sea Musketeers presentation just a few days later, I think it might be the best month out of this fabulous year. Maybe I could even wear a sash that says NEW CITIZEN to the city council meeting. That surely would help our case.

Mom starts to salsa in the living room and twirls me around.

Nick looks over at us from his spot on the couch. "I'd dance, too, but I've only got one good foot."

I snort. That's a joke. Nick never likes to salsa with us. He joins us only if we really beg.

"I've got even better news, too," Mom continues. "*Hablé con tus abuelos y* they are coming for the ceremony."

"Apolinar *and* Maria?" I'm shocked. Apolinar, *mi abuelo*, comes every year for Thanksgiving at least, but *mi abuela* hates traveling. I've only really seen her probably four times since I was a baby, and twice, we visited her. All I know is that she smells like gardenias, loves the music of Sarita Montiel, and makes a mean *sopa de fideos*.

Mom laughs. "Yup, the two of them. That's what I was discussing with Juanis on the phone last week. She's going to go stay with your *tía* Maria in Oaxaca while they come to visit us. Now that we have the date, I can book their flights."

"Whoa!" Nick says. "Well, good thing my cast

will be off by then." He looks at his newly marked-up cast.

Mom puts her hand on his shoulder to comfort him. She knows that he must be thinking about Apolinar. He always uses the crutches at night after he takes off his artificial leg. The visit would be harder for Apolinar if he and Nick had to share them.

Mom adds, "And they even renewed Maria's passport, so they are all set."

I frown a little. I start picturing my Mexican passport. I love it! It's green, and it has a hologram inside. However, if I become a United States citizen, I will have to give that up. I have never considered what I might be giving up in the process of becoming a citizen. It feels a little uncomfortable to lose that part of me.

I shake it off. Instead, I begin making a list of everywhere I want to take *mis abuelos*. First of all, we have to go to the Shedd Aquarium. I'll tell them about my summer camp and everything I learned there. Then I remember the fact that they don't speak English very well, and I speak *muy poco* Spanish. Mom and Nick always help me communicate with my grandparents, but it slows down the conversation.

I'm lost in my own thoughts until Mom interrupts them by saying, "*Niños*, we do have an urgent problem."

"What do you mean?" I reply, concerned.

"What do you all want to do for our weekly appointment?" She smiles.

I giggle with relief. Our weekly appointments happen every Friday night, and that's when we do something fun together as a family. I glance over at Nick. "Whatever Nick wants to do."

Nick thinks for a second and gets a mischievous look. "Chinese takeout and a horror movie with zombies."

I shudder. I hate scary movies, especially zombie ones. I either hide behind the couch or close my eyes while I plug my ears with my fingers. Still, I promised to make Nick happy, so I reluctantly nod.

He laughs. "I was only serious about the takeout. Let's find a movie we all want to watch."

I clasp my hands together. "Thank you, *hermano*."

Chapter Nine

We host the next Sea Musketeers meet-ing at Mariel's again. As Kristen and Logan work on the slideshow, I decide to tell Mariel my good news about my *abuelos* visiting.

"But they are like your *abuela*, where they don't speak much English," I say nervously.

Mariel clasps her hands together. "*¡Tengo una buena idea!*"

Before I can ask her what the great idea is, she blurts out, "What if we practice your Spanish together?"

I bite my lip. That's tempting, but it's a little scary. What if I sound horrible?

She gives me a gentle shove. "It'll be super fun, and I promise not to laugh."

I let out a small sigh of relief. "Okay, but . . . when do you think we can practice? They are coming in a month or so."

She taps her head as she thinks. "Why don't we meet half an hour before each meeting? I'll check with my parents, but I'm sure they will say yes."

"*Sí, por favor,*" I reply.

While Mariel checks with her parents, Stanley leans

over to me. "Is it okay if I make a non-presentation announcement?"

I nod.

Stanley speaks. "Hey, everyone. This is slightly off topic, but I received a new telescope for Christmas, and there is going to be a meteor shower next month that we will actually be able to see in Chicago. I wanted to know if you all want to come to my house to see it."

"Like a party?" Jenny asks excitedly.

"I guess so." He scratches his head. "It would be a space-viewing party."

Kristen replies, "I love parties. For my upcoming eleventh birthday, my mom promised me a pizza party and a spa day. I can choose any hairstyle I want."

Kristen smiles so wide you can see all her braces. I've never seen her without braids. I wonder if she'll let her hair loose like mine. Maybe puffy hair could be the official Sea Musketeers look for the presentation.

As the group continues to plan, I begin to day-dream about the presentation and what it might look like. Will it be a big room? Will there be many people?

All I know is I hope it goes well. The Sea Musketeers have been working toward this for months, and we've done a lot. We've had fundraisers, we've volunteered . . . not to mention how many people have signed our pledge. Close to a thousand! All together, our efforts have made a difference and helped our community.

Suddenly, my stomach flips like a giant humpback whale. But what if all this preparation is still not enough?

I wiggle my shoulders and squeeze my sea turtle. I don't want to take any chance of something going wrong in my best year. I will just have to try harder. Then I sit up straight and take as many notes as I can during the rest of the meeting.

Chapter Ten

Monday morning, Ms. Benedetto has a few of us share our personal wave stories aloud with the class. Chris volunteers to share, and to my surprise, his personal wave is not about his dad. It's when they moved to a new house! I scratch my head in disbelief when I hear that. I was positive I knew what he would write about. Then again, maybe it's so personal that he didn't want to share it with the group. Thankfully, Ms. Benedetto begins to speak.

"A big round of applause for everyone who shared." After we finish clapping, she says, "And now it's time for math, and I have a fun project lined up!"

I squeal. Ms. Benedetto is the best teacher. She

always has us do experiments where we get to work with our hands. Last fall, we even did an egg-drop project.

"This morning, we're going to make our own slime and practice our fractions with it."

"I just love slime!" exclaims Stanley.

I wholeheartedly agree. Slime is particularly fun since I just read that there are a few marine animals that produce their own slime. For instance, mandarinfish are covered in colorful slime to ward off predators. The slime basically says, *Hey, don't eat me! I'm poisonous!* That's pretty smart, if you ask me. Although being slime-covered might be gross if you are not in the ocean. Can you imagine how hard it would be to walk if everything you touched stuck to your body?

Ms. Benedetto motions for us to stand up. "Now gather around for the demo."

As we crowd around her, she shows us how to make the slime by pouring our three ingredients—baking soda, white glue, and contact solution—into a bowl.

It takes only a little mixing until it gets all sticky and gooey in her hands. She also has food coloring so we can make our slime any color we'd like.

Ms. Benedetto then says, "Now grab a partner and let's get started."

Usually, I would pair up with Jenny, but I do something impulsive. I make a dash toward Chris! This seems like the perfect opportunity to get to know him better and ask him more about his dad. Jenny looks shocked at first that I'm running away from her, but once she sees me approaching Chris, she nods to me. She works with Anna instead.

"Chris, do you want to be my partner?" I say, out of breath.

He looks up at me, a little surprised. "Uh, sure!"

Since we both like art, it takes a while to choose only one color for our slime. He wanted red and I wanted blue, so we compromise on purple. After our slime mixture goes from clumpy to gooey, Ms. Benedetto instructs us to begin practicing our fractions by pulling the slime into halves, fourths, and eighths.

While pulling the slime apart into halves, I struggle to think of what to say to Chris that isn't art related. To my surprise, he is quieter than I realized. When we're together in art club, we're usually busy, so I haven't paid attention. I also never noticed how deep in thought he looks. I wonder if he is sad. I guess I assumed that since his laugh and voice are so loud that he must be chatty all the time. I stare at the slime and resort to some of my conversation starters.

"What did you do this weekend?" I ask. Mom says that's a polite question to start with.

He stretches the slime far apart between his fingers and says, "I had piano practice, and we went to the movies."

"That's cool! I didn't know you play the piano," I reply.

He nods. "My parents thought it would be good for me, and it's actually really fun."

I wonder if they thought it would be good for him since I imagine it's so hard for him at home. I've heard that music can be therapeutic. Mom sometimes puts on spa music after a long day of work and asks for a little "*silencio*."

"Good for you?" I ask with a raised eyebrow.

He chuckles. "It helps me sit still and focus. I can be hyperactive."

"Oh," I reply. He's quiet and hyperactive? I want to ask him more, especially about his dad, but Ms. Benedetto announces that it is break time. I walk back to my seat with more questions about Chris than before, but I don't want to be pushy. I better wait till tomorrow.

When I get back home after school, Nick is working at the dining room table. He lifts his head from his homework and says, "Linda called, and she asked if you could walk Biscuit. She had to run some errands."

I squeal. I relish any extra time with Biscuit during the week.

He shakes his head. "I will take that as a yes. I'll let her know."

I nod and zip up my coat to go next door. Since there is no snow on the ground, I don't have to put little booties on Biscuit, just a warm jacket. As I walk him around the street, I am reminded of my resolutions. By walking Biscuit, I am one step closer to proving to Mom that I would be a responsible dog owner. I mentally add a check to that goal in my head. I also know being helpful to Linda is part of my citizenship goals, which means I get another check. But I wonder, does Biscuit think I'm being helpful to him, too? I bend down, and before I can speak, he greets me with a lick on the nose.

"Check number three!" I whisper.

After I return Biscuit home, and with our citizenship on my mind, I decide to talk to Nick about our ceremony.

"Nick, are you excited about becoming a citizen?"

He puts his textbook down. "Yeah, I think so, but . . . I mean, it's different for me."

"What do you mean?" I ask, puzzled.

He leans back in his chair. "You were just a baby when we moved here, but I was almost seven and in school. I remember leaving Mexico, saying goodbye to friends, and then us starting over. Then having to take ESL classes for a couple of months. So . . ." He pauses. "While I think it's awesome that we're getting our citizenship, it still feels a little bit weird. Does that make sense?"

I nod. In many ways, I have always felt Nick is more Mexican than me. Namely because he remembers living in Mexico. Nick also speaks Spanish with our *abuelos* without a problem. They even babysat him after school! So if he's worried about feeling less Mexican and I'm already less than him, what does that make me? Maybe I can use the math I learned today at school. If Mom is full Mexican, then is Nick half Mexican? Then does that make me a quarter Mexican? *Gulp*, negative Mexican? I don't like the math in this formula.

Chapter Eleven

At our next art club meeting, we work on another set of self-portraits. We've done a couple more since our imaginative drawings. Unlike the previous times, we have to use a mirror today to draw our self-portraits. The strange thing is we can't look at our paper at all while we draw.

Ms. Benedetto explains, "This type of drawing is called a blind contour."

"But won't we mess up?" asks Anna.

Mr. Foster replies, "Don't worry about that. This method of drawing helps you train your eye. That way, you learn to observe all the details instead of just staring at your paper. Sometimes we draw what we think we see instead of what is actually there."

While we begin to sketch, we also have our individual meetings with Ms. Benedetto. It's time to share our ideas for the portraits and turn in our permission slips for the field trip. As much as I try to focus on my blind contour, I'm feeling impatient to tell her who I've selected for the gallery show. When she finally calls my name, I walk over excitedly. After I hand in my permission slip, she asks, "Stella, whom have you decided to draw for the portrait?"

"Mr. Don."

She writes it down into her notepad. "I think he'll really appreciate that. You know, we might be able to take his picture now. I'll call you back over if I can get him in here. If not, I'll definitely make sure he is available for the next meeting."

I practically skip back to my spot next to Chris. He's almost in a trance, staring intensely at the mirror. Today I am determined to ask him about his dad and PLS. When Anna gets called up from our table to talk to Ms. Benedetto, it's just me and him, and I think now might be the right time.

As I get back to work on my drawing, I muster up the courage to discuss it with him.

"Chris?"

"Yes?" he replies, still drawing.

"Um . . . Stanley told me why your dad is in a wheelchair," I say.

As Chris drops his pencil, the corners of his mouth lower down, too. "Yeah, PLS is not a great thing to have."

"Has your dad always had it?" I ask.

Chris shakes his head. "He started showing symptoms when I was in kindergarten. At least that's what they tell me. All I know is he used to be my team's soccer coach, then one day he suddenly had to stop. It's gotten worse since then, but thankfully it's slowed down."

"I also saw that there was no cure," I say.

Chris glances around to see if anyone is looking. "Stella, can we not talk about it now?"

"Yes. I'm sorry."

I then mimic zipping my mouth shut. As much as I want to ask him more, I can tell it's upsetting him. Maybe it would be better to bring it up later when we're completely by ourselves. Instead, I look over at his drawing. While not everything is exactly in the right spot, it really does look like Chris.

"Wow, your drawing looks so great!"

Chris looks down at it and grins. Then he peeks over at mine. "Yours does, too."

I stare down at the paper. He's not lying. It actually does! Except that one of my eyes is where my nose should be. It almost looks like a flounder. They are famous for being asymmetrical. I look over at the clock. My portrait is pretty much finished, but we still have a bit longer before we go home.

I ask, "Do you want to draw each other?"

"Oh, can I join you two?" Anna asks as she walks back to the table.

The three of us begin to draw each other blind-contour style. Usually I don't enjoy staring at people for

this long because I turn *roja*. But this is different. It's captivating, like looking at an aquarium. I could stare at an aquarium for hours, watching the variety of sea creatures swim by. Who knew that eyebrows and freckles could be just as fascinating? While we're drawing, Ms. Benedetto taps on my shoulder.

"Mr. Don is here. Do you want to take a picture of him now? I have it all ready, so you just have to click the button."

I jump up and see him standing by the door. He waves at me. I can see Ms. Benedetto has set up the camera on a tripod. I grab my notebook and walk over to him.

He says, "I'm so flattered, Stella. Thank you for asking me to be a part of the project."

"You're welcome!" I reply shyly.

Ms. Benedetto gets him to sit down in a chair in front of the tripod and leaves to help Mr. Foster. I direct Mr. Don to turn his head and smile. I try a mixture of poses like smiling and unsmiling pictures. As he sits there, I slyly open up my notebook.

"Mr. Don, do you mind if I ask you a few questions?"

He replies, "No problem!"

I trace my finger to the first question on the page. "Do you like being an American citizen?"

He sticks his chest out proudly. "Of course! I now get to vote, which is very important."

"That's true," I reply. Then I say softly, "But do you ever worry that you're less Filipino now?"

Mr. Don shakes his head and looks at me. "Are you worried about that, Stella?"

I nod. "But I don't want to say anything to my mom about it, because I don't want to sound like I'm not grateful."

He gives me a reassuring smile.

"In my opinion, I don't think that I have lost anything by becoming a citizen. In fact, I have only gained another culture and opportunities."

I start to relax. When he phrases it like that, I feel a little less worried. I skim down the page in my notebook to my next question.

"How was the actual ceremony? What happens?"

"It was wonderful!" He pauses and looks away as if he is remembering. "I even cried!"

"Really?" That must be very special. Grown-ups cry in public only at weddings, funerals, and sad movies. Like when Mom bawled at the movie *Coco*.

He nods. "I dressed up for it, and my entire family was there. But I guess what made me emotional was the moment after you receive the citizenship certificates. All the new citizens recited a pledge together. Just seeing this whole group united, well . . . it was memorable. That's when you really become part of the USA."

My whole face erupts into a smile, but I immediately pull back. While this is thrilling, I can't get too excited until the actual ceremony. Only then is it truly official.

Ms. Benedetto then comes back to check on us.

"Are you all done here?"

I reply. "Yup! Thanks, Mr. Don."

He gives me an elbow tap. "You're welcome, Stella. Can't wait to see your drawing."

On the car ride home with Chris, I make sure not to mention his father to him again. I decide I want to wait till I have a solution, a cure, or some way to help him. That way he'll be happy and not upset. And I finally think I know a good place to start.

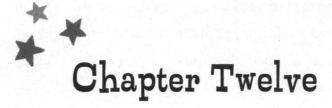

Chapter Twelve

Saturday morning, I go over to Linda's to walk Biscuit. This is my chance to ask her more about my lucky sea turtle. After talking to Chris this week, I believe his dad could use one, too. She always takes a moment to chat with me before her book club. This time, we're chatting as she sets up her computer on the dining room table. Her sister in Wisconsin joins the book club virtually over video.

"What book are you reading this time?" I ask, clipping the leash onto Biscuit's harness.

"We're in the middle of this crime series. They are intense!" she replies, wiggling her shoulders in suspense.

I wince. I feel the same way about crime novels as I do about horror and zombies. *No me gusta.*

"Linda, where did you get my sea turtle figurine exactly? What store?"

She replies, "It was at a gift shop on the island. I don't know the name."

"Oh." The Bahamas seems really far away, and without a name, it might be hard to find the store.

She looks at me curiously. "How come, sugarplum?"

"I just have a friend who could use some good luck, and I wanted to get him one."

"Isn't that sweet," she replies. "I'll be right back."

She opens her hallway closet door and reaches into a storage container, pulling out another small box.

"I bought a few extra as gifts. Here, you can give him this one."

I squeal. "Really?" I can't believe she has had all this magic in her closet this entire time.

She hands me the sea turtle. It's identical to my own except it's a slightly darker shade of tan.

I give her a big hug.

"He is sure lucky to have you as a friend," Linda remarks.

After I walk Biscuit, I head back to my house. I feel pretty special. I'm walking around with two lucky sea turtles! Imagine what I could do with this much luck. Maybe I should have Mom play the lottery, but I ignore that urge. That would be selfish and not an example of good citizenship. I'll make sure to give it to Chris soon—like during our field trip next week!

When I get back, Nick is curled up on the couch with his foot on the ottoman. His cast is covered in even more signatures than before. It looks like we started a trend. There is hardly a blank spot left.

This time, instead of doing homework, he is playing video games on his phone. Now that he can't work or take karate lessons, Nick's been playing them even more than usual. Lately, he reminds me of a nurse shark, barely moving. He usually plays with his best friend, Jason, and other kids he's met online.

I sometimes sit by him and draw sea creatures when

he plays his video games, but today I'm busy. I've got my Sea Musketeers meeting. I lean over to him.

"Can I get you anything? I know . . . how about another chocolate milk?"

He stares at the screen and presses the buttons. "Do you have the ability to speed up healing or time?"

I put my hand on my face. "Not that I know of."

"Then I want nothing," he replies, still staring at his phone.

I try harder. "Cheer up, Nick. You're at the halfway mark and you've only got one more month to go. Even though the groundhog didn't see his shadow, it's still cold outside. You don't want to be out there."

He pauses his game and looks at me. "Right now, I'd take subzero temperatures and arctic wind chills if it meant I could go walk outside and do something other than homework and video games."

Then he resumes the game. I frown. Apparently, I'm not helping him today as much as I would like. I come up with another idea.

"Do you want to come to my Sea Musketeers meeting? It's at our house today. You could help us with our presentation as our unofficial mentor."

He taps the screen harder. "No. Hanging out with a bunch of kids doesn't sound like fun."

I hear a message ding on his phone. He pauses the game to look while I stomp away. Mom must have heard the conversation, because she stops me in the kitchen.

"He doesn't mean it. Nick's just frustrated. Give him some space. He'll be in a better mood soon. *Te lo prometo*."

I silently nod, but inside, every part of me disagrees. Clearly, I'm just not trying hard enough. I'm determined to figure out a way to brighten his mood, but then the doorbell rings—it must be Mariel, here early to practice Spanish with me. While I like practicing with Mom, she usually is too busy with work to do it as often as I'd like. I'm also a little shy to ask her for help. At least Mariel understands what it's like to be confused between two languages.

We head to the kitchen. "What is something you'd like to ask your *abuelos*?" Mariel says. She is sitting on the other side of the kitchen table and looks very much like a teacher.

My mind goes blank. There is so much that I want to say, but I guess maybe I should start with the most basic question.

"Did you have a good flight?"

Mariel translates, "*¿Tuviste un buen vuelo?* Now you try."

I wince and repeat back nervously, "Too-ve-ste oon bwen voo-loh?"

"Not bad." She gives me a thumbs-up. She then passes me a book from her bag. I pick it up and read the title: *The Everything Kids' Learning Spanish Book*.

"I found it in the used bookstore. My parents said it might help if we do some of the exercises in the book."

I clasp my hands. *"Bueno idea."*

She whispers, "It's *buena idea*."

"Oops . . . ," I reply, and then mutter, "Spanish can be hard."

We work on some of the puzzles where we have to match up the phrases with the pictures. At first, I feel embarrassed. The illustrations look as if the book is for little kids. I'm smarter than a preschooler, but I guess not in Spanish. I try to push that *roja* feeling aside. It takes a while, but the puzzles end up being kind of fun. I'd give myself a grade of two and half sea stars out of five sea stars.

Before I know it, the rest of the Sea Musketeers show up for the meeting. After I take attendance, Stanley hands out invitations to his space party.

"It's in one month. The weekend before the city council presentation."

"A perfect way to relax," Kristen replies.

We begin drafting out who will speak first during the presentation.

"I think I should go first," says Logan, holding the toy orca.

I want to say no, but I take a breath. He's the copresident and I should be open.

Thankfully, Stanley grabs the orca. "I think Stella should go first. This is sort of her big idea. What if you go in the middle, Logan? That way you can really spice it up and make sure no one gets bored."

"I guess I could do that." Logan looks proud. "I'll liven things back up."

While we work in my room, I hear another voice in the house. It sounds like a girl, but older than me. Maybe it's Izzy? While everyone is hard at work adding the finishing touches to the slideshow, I make an excuse to grab a snack for the group and walk downstairs to inspect. To my surprise, I see Nick sitting next to a girl his age. I tiptoe to the kitchen first, where Mom helps me fill up a big bowl with popcorn and pretzels. Then I walk back loudly through the living room. The new girl smiles when she sees me.

"Is that your sister? She's got awesome curls."

Nick nods while I turn *roja*. While I do love my curls, I always hate it when people talk about me as if I weren't in the room.

"Yeah, that's Stella. She's having a group meeting with her friends that she needs to get back to."

He motions at me to leave the room, but the girl stands up to greet me. I squint my eyes. She seems familiar. I wonder if it's Nick's homecoming date, Erika. I've never met her, but he showed us pictures afterward.

"Isn't that sweet? Well, I'm Erika. I just came over to work on some homework with your brother and bring him some cookies."

I wave back. Then I watch Nick take a bite of a cookie.

In between bites, he says, "These are my favorite, too."

I examine the bin full of cookies. I expect to see the no-bake peanut butter kind, but they're not there. It's not even the kind with chocolate candies. These are plain old sugar cookies, which Nick and I agree are the most boring of all the cookies. Of course, I don't say anything aloud. A good citizen is always courteous.

"Nice to meet you, Erika," I reply.

However, I'm upset inside. I offered Nick all the

things that usually make him happy just an hour earlier, but none of it brightened his mood. Why did Erika make him so much happier than me? Am I not trying hard enough?

I head back to the meeting, determined to be better.

Chapter Thirteen

Tap. Tap. Tap.

Ms. Charlton keeps the rhythm with her foot on the floor while the dance class moves around the room.

It's after school, and I'm sitting in the corner of the dance studio. I'm watching Jenny's dance class rehearse for their upcoming competition. Jenny's mom had to run a few errands, so she left me to watch Jenny instead of dropping me back at home first. I don't mind at all. I love watching Jenny dance because she's simply amazing. When Jenny performs, she moves around as if she were a mermaid in the ocean.

Then I hear Ms. Charlton say, "Jenny, make sure to land that jump on the beat."

Jenny glances over to me. She is frowning. I give her a thumbs-up as a sign of encouragement. I mouth, "You can do it."

Ms. Charlton says, "Let's do this again from the very beginning."

I watch carefully as Jenny's group performs again. This time when Jenny lands the jump perfectly, her teacher comments.

"Well done!"

After her class, Jenny runs up to me covered in sweat. It's so much sweat that you'd almost think she just went swimming.

"Did I look okay? I messed up in that one spot." She fiddles with her bun anxiously.

"AMAZING. Ms. Charlton seems really tough on you. You're the best one in the group."

Jenny beams. "Really?"

I nod. "Don't forget you can borrow my sea turtle, too, for the competition this weekend."

I throw my arm around her. Even though she feels like a wet fish, I can see she needs some extra encouragement.

"Thanks, bestie."

This makes me feel better. While I may need to work on my citizenship skills with Nick, at least I can be a good, supportive best friend. Let's just hope I am as helpful to Chris tomorrow.

The next morning, I prepare for my Art Institute field trip. I check my list and carefully pack up my backpack. I make sure to bring my recently sharpened colored pencils and a fresh composition book just in case I get an opportunity to draw. Then I pack the lunch Mom made me. She usually includes a special treat on field trip days. Finally, I make sure to bring my extra sea turtle with me for Chris.

I can't wait to see his face when I give it to him. I've

been brainstorming other ways to help his dad, too. I'm optimistic that it is going to be a great day. Maybe one of the top ten of the year.

On the way to school, Mom asks me from the front seat, "Are you excited, Stella?"

"I almost can't contain it," I reply, tapping my feet. "I get to go to the Art Institute *and* during a school day. That's so exciting!"

Outside of the school building, Mom stops the car. She grabs a few dollars from her wallet and passes them to me from the front seat.

"Here's a little money if you'd like to buy a souvenir. They sell postcards of artwork in the museum store. You might need one for your portrait assignment."

I squeal. "Thank you!"

I unbuckle my seat belt and lean forward to give her a kiss on the cheek.

On the way to the museum, I sit near Chris and Anna in our small school bus. Mr. Foster and Ms. Benedetto were able to get a grant for our trip, which means we were able to get not only free tickets, but also transportation. As much as I want to give Chris his present right now, I know he is sensitive about talking about his dad. I decide to wait until we are alone to give him the sea turtle.

After Ms. Benedetto and Mr. Foster check our group in at the museum, we begin a tour with a guide. They take us through many exhibits to see a variety of famous works. The beautiful stained-glass windows by Marc Chagall make my mouth drop. We also see a painting of an unhappy man holding a pitchfork, with his daughter beside him, in front of a barn.

"I don't think they were having a great day," I say to myself.

Then we see the two best exhibits of the tour. The first is the Thorne miniature gallery. There are sixty-eight tiny rooms that you can peek inside. Each is a complete replica of a historic room, just doll-size. How

I wish I could shrink myself down and go inside one! The second is when I finally see the Vincent van Gogh self-portrait. The rippling brushstrokes look more dramatic in person than they do in a photograph. He looks a little sadder in person, too. I'll just have to make sure not to draw Mr. Don with that expression.

Next, Ms. Benedetto and Mr. Foster spilt us up into two smaller groups so we can spend some time with individual paintings for inspiration. I make sure to stand next to Chris so that I end up in the same group with him. Ms. Benedetto takes the other group to the modern-art wing while Mr. Foster takes our group around the Postimpressionist room. There are so many beautiful paintings to stare at, but then I notice Chris standing alone in front of a painting. When I get close, I see that he is admiring a still life of apples by Paul Cézanne. This is my chance. I take the second sea turtle out of my pencil bag and walk over.

"Cool painting."

He replies, "Definitely."

"I brought you a present, Chris."

"Really?" He turns toward me, looking excited. This is going just like I imagined.

I pull out the sea turtle from the box and hand it to him.

"Wow!" he whispers, and holds it in his hands. "I like how it's carved. Thank you, Stella!"

I take a deep breath. "It's supposed to bring good luck, and I thought it might help your dad."

Chris's expression quickly changes. "What do you mean?" He sounds a little short.

"Well, I just thought maybe it could help bring a cure. I have a sea turtle just like that one, and it's brought me great luck this year. I just wanted you all to have some good luck, too."

He stares at me silently.

I continue, "And I'd be happy to do fundraising to help. I do it all the time for the Sea Musketeers."

He suddenly frowns. All my surprises don't seem to be going over well. I kept picturing that he'd give me a big hug at least. Maybe he'd even shed a tear or two of joy. Instead, it looks like he is trying not to get upset.

He hands the sea turtle back to me.

"I don't believe in good luck or magic. You can have your gift back."

I'm shocked. "I'm sorry, Chris. I just want to help."

He nods and walks away. I squeeze the sea turtle in my hand.

Throughout the rest of our field trip, I try talking to him a few times, but he keeps avoiding me in the exhibits and even in the museum store.

After the Art Institute, we have lunch near a giant reflective sculpture known to everyone in Chicago as the Bean. The sculpture is actually called *Cloud Gate*, but it looks like a moon jellyfish to me. That aquatic image doesn't make me feel better. I eat my cold sunflower butter sandwich by myself. It doesn't taste as good as it normally does. Neither does the special treat from my mom, my Carlos V chocolate bar.

I stare as Chris chats with Anna and a couple of the other art club members. All I wanted to do was help Chris and help his dad, but it seems as if it's not working. I don't understand. What did I do wrong?

And who doesn't want good luck? Maybe it's that my citizenship skills are lacking. As much as I've tried, I've failed both Nick and Chris lately. I hope I can figure out this mystery soon before my ceremony and, more importantly, before I lose a new friend forever.

Chapter Fourteen

Today is one of our final Sea Musketeers meetings before we present in front of the city council. Like the past few weeks, Mariel and I practice my Spanish before the meeting. As we wrap up our session, she asks me, "*¿Como te sientes con tu español?*"

"*Mejor*," I reply, and it's the truth, too. The more I speak it, the less frustrated I feel. All the practice is actually working! It's almost as if I'm using all these words and phrases that have been stuck in my brain. Words that I remember my family saying to me. I find myself surprised at times that I know how to respond. It makes me more excited about *mis abuelos* visiting. Better yet, it distracts me from how I felt this past week. I can't find a reason why Chris got upset with me at the Art Institute.

Soon the rest of the Sea Musketeers show up, and we begin practicing our verbal presentation. I can tell from how little everyone is joking that we are all feeling the pressure of the big event.

I read from the note cards I worked on at home. Mom even helped me revise my presentation, so I would sound more grown-up. We also made sure it was all words that I can pronounce easily.

"Hello, members of the city council. We're the Sea Musketeers, an organization of students committed to protecting the oceans. We're concerned about the growing plastic problem in our oceans, which is why we created a pledge to cut back on plastics. We're here today to talk about adopting this pledge at all of our schools."

Kristen says, "That sounds great. Maybe speak a little louder?"

"I think there will be a microphone," I reply, a little sharply.

While I know she means well, I hate being told to speak louder. It's a problem I've always had. My voice always sounds plenty loud in my head.

"Maybe you can say how our club name is inspired by Jacques Cousteau and his group of friends?" suggests Logan.

I make a note of this on my note card. I'm a little discouraged because I worked hard on my introduction. I was expecting the Sea Musketeers to love it, but from the sound of it, I may have to spend some more time on it.

"And look up more from the cards," says Jenny with a smile.

I remember when Jessica presented her animal project in third grade. She read from her cards the whole time, so I know firsthand it's not a great look during a presentation. However, when the stakes are this high, it's hard not to want to look at my notes.

I nod. The group is right and only trying to help. "I'll work on memorizing it."

Thankfully, Kristen interrupts. "I know we shouldn't be talking about anything else, but did you guys hear there might be a blizzard next week?"

"How? It's like fifty degrees today!" Mariel exclaims. "And we're only a couple weeks away from spring."

"Winter lasts a really long time in Chicago. It's not like Miami, where winter ends right away," says Logan. Unlike Mariel, he's a native of Chicago.

Mariel moved to Chicago last summer, so she's still getting used to the colder weather. She misses the warmer temperatures, but she likes being able to accessorize with beanies, gloves, and scarves. I wonder what she'll think when she experiences a really strong cold snap with winds that practically knock you over!

"I hope that doesn't mess with our presentation or

my space party. This meteor shower rarely happens," says Stanley.

"I'm sure it won't," I reply.

I pull out my pencil bag to find my sea turtle and give it a quick squeeze, but I can't find it with my fingers. I practically put my whole head in there to search for it, but no luck. Then I start frantically touching my pockets.

"What's wrong, Stella?" asks Logan.

I begin to say in my fake-calm voice, "I'm just looking for . . . ," when I spy the sea turtle on the table next to my journal. I grab it and sigh. "Oh, never mind."

Chris may not think that good-luck charms do anything, but I know mine works. In fact, I am so confident that I lent Chris's sea turtle to Jenny in the meantime. She has her dance competition today after the meeting. If Jenny earns a ribbon, that might be the proof Chris needs to convince him that it actually works.

Kristen raises her hands to her face. "Can you imagine if we'd have to reschedule because of the blizzard?"

We all fall silent. This would definitely be a blow to

our crusade. Not to mention this meeting has already been rescheduled once.

Stanley shakes his head. "We can't focus on that. Let's keep rehearsing."

Logan nods. "He's right. Who's next?"

After our meeting, I work on the portrait of Mr. Don back at home. It's due this week for the gallery show. I tried using pastels to draw the portrait in the last club meeting, but my fingers got too messy and I sneezed from the chalk powder. Instead, after many studies, I settle on colored pencils to make the swirly marks to draw the final portrait. I keep my postcard of Vincent van Gogh's portrait nearby while I draw from the photograph. Mom comes by my room to check on me.

"*¡Mi amor, es increíble!*" she says, examining my drawing.

"Really?" I turn around and look at her.

"I promise. It's beautiful. I'm so proud of you."

She tousles my hair.

"I've been thinking that we should buy new outfits for the citizenship ceremony. Nothing super fancy, but

this will happen once in our life. We should look nice for the photos."

I nod. "Remember, that's what Mr. Don said. He and his family dressed up for the ceremony."

"Then we must go shopping."

I beam. Just hearing about the ceremony lightens my mood. It makes me forget about a potential blizzard and the fact Chris isn't speaking to me.

"I want to get a red-and-blue outfit," I reply. "That way I will look like a great citizen."

Then I remember something else Mr. Don told me. "Oh, and can we print out the citizenship oath, too? I want to practice."

"*¡Claro que sí!* I'll print it out on Monday at work and then we can go shopping when I get home."

I throw my arms around her. "*¡Perfecto!*"

She grabs my hand. "Let's go check on your brother. I think he may be less grumpy today. He's only got a week or so left on his cast."

I walk with Mom downstairs. I can't wait till my brother has his cast off. Once it is gone, I won't have to worry about him being happy. It's been sort of exhausting worrying about him and trying to keep him upbeat. Not to mention, Nick will be able to walk with me after school again. Then it won't be so bad if Chris is still giving me the silent treatment, because I'll be with Nick.

I cross my arms in determination. Cast or no cast, I don't want to give up on working things out with Chris.

Chapter Fifteen

I bring my finished portrait of Mr. Don to school on Tuesday for our art club meeting. I was dying to show Ms. Benedetto in class all day, but I managed to wait until just before the start of the meeting.

I stand by her desk in suspense while she examines my drawing quietly. Then she looks at me with a proud expression.

"It's wonderful, Stella. Mr. Don is going to be so impressed."

I grin.

She tucks my portrait away. "Next time you see it, it will be hung up on the wall for everyone to see at parent-teacher night."

Chris shows up behind me, carrying a portfolio case like a professional artist. He pulls out his portrait and hands it to Ms. Benedetto. It is the best thing I've ever seen him do. I'm so impressed by all the polka dots he included.

"I love it!" I say. Chris gives me a smile the size of a plankton. Trust me, that is tiny. A blue whale has to eat eight thousand pounds of them a day just to feel full.

Not actual size

With a smile that small, I can tell he still doesn't want to talk to me.

Ms. Benedetto praises his drawing as well before storing it away. Back at our table, I keep trying to talk to Chris, but he doesn't respond much. I try to tell him that Jenny won second place at the competition and she had a lucky sea turtle with her. But he keeps talking to Anna instead.

On the way home, he continues the mostly silent treatment. It's been this way for the past week or so.

I've managed to distract Mrs. Pollard by asking her questions about being a graphic designer and sharing my conversation starters, but today I officially give up.

She notices the silence, because she asks, "Are you okay, Chris? You're not talking much."

"I'm fine. Just sleepy," he replies. It seems like he hasn't mentioned anything to his mom.

She glances at him in the rearview mirror. "You're probably just hungry. I'll fix you a snack when we get home."

"Thanks, Mom," he says as he looks out the window.

At the stoplight, she continues, "I picked up the apples and cheddar that you like, too. Your father was craving it after his swim."

My mouth drops. I say without thinking, "Your dad can swim? But how?"

Chris's mom turns around and looks at me. "Chris's dad loves to swim!"

I raise my eyebrows in shock.

She must have noticed, because then she says, "Being in a wheelchair just means you have to do some things differently." She looks forward again and continues, "It doesn't mean you can't do anything."

"I didn't know that," I reply softly.

"Neither did we until we experienced it firsthand," she replies. "Now we manage it pretty well. Right, Chris?"

Chris nods and then looks out the window again.

I'm starting to realize there is much I don't understand about Chris's family and his dad. I think I've been very wrong before about them.

Two days later, we have our parent-teacher night. It's always so exciting because I get to explore the school with Mom at night. It's almost like when she takes me around her office, except there aren't the cool vending machines with honey buns at my school.

Mom is still dressed in her work clothes, so she looks like a *jefa*. It always makes me so proud. Even though it might be nice if I had a dad who would

121

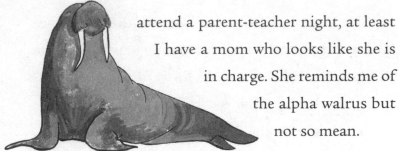

attend a parent-teacher night, at least I have a mom who looks like she is in charge. She reminds me of the alpha walrus but not so mean.

I show Mom the hallways and lead her to our gallery show. She playfully elbows me. "Yours is one of the best ones up there."

I turn *roja* and then I notice something exciting. "Look, Mom, they framed one of our self-portraits, too!"

Beside the portrait of Mr. Don is the first self-portrait, where I drew completely from my imagination. I look around and see Chris's work.

Mom points at his blind-contour self-portrait. "This one is pretty great. Hard to believe a child did it."

I'm about to say it's Chris's drawing when someone says, "Thank you."

I turn around. To my surprise, it's Chris's dad. At least I think it is, because it is a man in a wheelchair, and he's right next to Chris's drawing. There is so much that I want to say, but I don't want to overwhelm him since this is the first time I am meeting him.

"I'm Stella," I say shyly.

"Oh, Chris's friend," he replies slowly. "He talks . . . about you."

Some of his words are a little hard to understand at first, and it takes me a second to hear what he says. When I do, I feel embarrassed. I hope Chris didn't tell his dad that he hates me. I was only trying to help him.

He wheels closer to the wall to inspect. "Which is yours?"

I point out my drawing of Mr. Don.

"Terrific," he replies as he examines the drawing. "Like . . . Van Gogh."

"That's what I was going for!" I exclaim.

Mom waves her hand to introduce herself. "I'm Perla. Stella's mom. It's very nice to meet you."

"I'm Robert," he replies, waving back.

Mom looks down at her watch. "It's my time to chat with Ms. Benedetto. Do you want to wait here, Stella?"

I nod. It will give me a moment to talk to Chris's dad.

When Mom leaves, it's just us. I stare at him, but I'm not quite sure what to say. I don't want to be rude or come across as not helpful.

Thankfully, he starts speaking. "Wondering . . . about this?" He points to his wheelchair.

I turn *roja*. I realize I had been staring at the chair more than his face. "Yes."

"Some . . . say it's bad luck . . ."

I can tell he struggles at times to get the words out, but that doesn't stop him. He just pauses and continues.

"But I don't believe it. It's just . . . what happened." Then he shrugs.

Hearing him speak, I can maybe understand why Chris didn't want the good-luck charm. His family doesn't believe in them.

"But don't you wish it were different?" I ask.

He nods. "Yes, but I'm . . . grateful. I get to work from home. Spend time with Chris."

"Oh," I reply.

As I look at his grinning face, I realize that he's completely different than I expected. He's not helpless. In fact, there is so much he is able to do. He can swim and work, and more importantly, he's happy. He also sounds like a great dad who knows plenty about art.

"Chris is lucky . . ." He leans in. "To have a friend . . . who cares."

I try to smile, but deep down, I feel the absolute worst. I haven't been a great friend to Chris lately. All

Chris wanted was my friendship, but all I've been doing is pushing unasked help onto him. That is the opposite of caring. In fact, it's mean. Even if it was unintentional. The more I think about it, the more I feel *roja* from the inside out—from my heart all the way to my tippy-toes.

Chris walks over to us with his mom. I can tell from his expression that he is not exactly pleased that I'm talking to his dad.

His dad points at me. "Stella is a . . . talented young lady."

Chris nods reluctantly.

It's silent for a second. Luckily, Stanley runs over to check out the show. He stops and drops his arms by his side.

"Whoa! This looks so cool!"

Mom and Ms. Benedetto walk over, too. Their meeting must be over. As Ms. Benedetto looks at the gallery wall, she says, "I have to admit I was sort of surprised that no one drew me, but they all turned out wonderfully."

I gasp. She's right! Among all twenty portraits, there isn't a single drawing of her. I see Ms. Morales, Coach Sullivan, and even Mrs. Hsu, but no Ms. Benedetto.

I exclaim, "I thought everyone was going to choose you!"

"Me too!" shouts Chris.

She giggles. "No worries. It's a fine show, and all these teachers and staff deserve to be recognized."

I lean over to Chris. While I want to apologize for being pushy, I'll save that conversation for later. For now, I have an idea that I think he might agree with. I whisper, "Hey, what if we all do a secret portrait of Ms. Benedetto?"

"Good idea," he replies. "My mom has all the parents' emails. We could send an email out letting everyone know."

He smiles for a second, but then he stops, probably when he remembers he is annoyed with me.

I ignore that and say, "Awesome. Let's bring them to the next art club meeting. That way we can surprise her."

He nods.

As we leave the building, I feel a little relieved. Talking to Chris's dad just helped put things into perspective. I also think I have an opportunity to make things right again with Chris with this secret Ms. Benedetto project.

Suddenly, there is a strong gust of wind, and it feels icy cold—like blizzard weather.

"We better check that weather report again," Mom says, rubbing her hands together. Then we walk quickly back home.

Chapter Sixteen

"I think a blizzard is coming our way," says Nick. He's reclining on the couch in his pajamas while watching the Saturday-morning news on television. Nick has been sitting there so often the past few weeks that there is now a semi-permanent Nick impression on the couch. He even keeps a wooden spoon nearby on the coffee table in case he has an itch under his cast.

I walk over to see what he is talking about.

"No way." I shake my head and stomp my foot. "It just can't! We have so many things planned. Your cast comes off, there's my presentation, and Apolinar and Maria are flying here tomorrow for our ceremony on Monday."

Nick shrugs. "Well, I don't know what to tell you. That's what the morning news said. If you want to call the meteorologists and complain, I'm sure they will listen."

I cross my arms. Right now is not the time for jokes.

Mom chimes in. "A blizzard doesn't have to mean an epic amount of snow. It will probably just snow a few feet by tomorrow, and then we'll be back to normal by the afternoon."

"That's not what the news says," Nick replies.

"But I have my Sea Musketeers meeting today. Not to mention Stanley's space party tonight."

Mom watches the news carefully. I can tell from her expression that she's growing concerned.

"We might need to postpone your activities, Stella. Let's check with your club members' parents and see what they want to do."

I stick my bottom lip as far out as it goes, but Mom ignores me. She's too busy planning.

"We should also go to the grocery store and get some extra food just in case."

We make phone calls to everyone in the club. Everyone's parents agreed that we should postpone the meeting till at least tomorrow. I guess it's not so terrible since we were just going to rehearse our city council presentation for the last time. At least that's what I tell myself.

Mom also suggested waiting to cancel on the space party. I let Stanley know over the phone that I might not be able to attend. He sounds a little disappointed, but he understands.

After the many phone calls, Mom and I finally head to the grocery store.

Nick shouts from the couch before we close the door, "Bring home some donuts, please!"

Mom gives me a long look and then throws her arm around me.

"I don't know about you, but I can't wait till he has that cast off."

I giggle a little, then I look up at the sky. It looks a bit gray and overcast, but there is no snow yet.

When we arrive at the grocery store, the parking lot

is packed as tightly as a school of sardines. Mom even has to drive the car around a few times before we can find a parking space. We grab our tote bags and head inside. I shiver as we walk toward the entrance. It does feel like it's getting colder.

Mom zips up her jacket. "Your brother might have to wait on donuts. It's a zoo in here."

We walk up and down the aisles, looking for bread, milk, and the other basics, but it's slim pickings. As I look around, I see people pushing carts overflowing with food and toilet paper. People are also acting a little rude and not like good citizens either. I feel nervous at the sight of all the chaos.

"*No tengas miedo.*" Mom tells me not to be afraid. She explains, "People just panic whenever there is bad weather. This always happens."

Still, we stare at our sad cart. There is only oat milk, which we usually never drink, and cinnamon-raisin bread. While it might be nice to try new things, I wish we had our regular food in our cart. Suddenly, she perks up.

"Let's get out of here. I've got a better place we can go."

We put back our two items and leave the long lines. To my surprise, Mom drives us to La Sorpresa. It's the Latin American grocery store. We usually go there for special treats, but they have all the regular groceries, too. Thankfully, it's much calmer inside.

"You're so *inteligente*," I tell her as we pick up our regular milk, bread, and cheese, plus some fun foods.

Mom nods.

"I was going to stop by anyway for *tus abuelos*. You know how your *abuelo* likes his papaya in the morning."

She grabs extra Abuelita hot chocolate and a treat for my brother called a Gansito. It's a chocolate-covered piece of cake with strawberry-jam filling. My favorite part is that it has a picture of an adorable duck on the outside.

"I don't remember the duck wearing clothes," I say, staring at the package.

"It's a *gansito*. A baby goose." She looks at it more carefully. "It was cuter before. Hopefully it tastes the same."

I reply, "Whatever it is, it's not a donut, but it will have to do."

As we leave the store and drive home, I remember the other blizzards we have had in the past. The one last October was so much fun, and it really lasted only a day. However, we've also had blizzards where we have been stuck at home for a few days and the electricity even goes out.

I really hope that is not the case. So much is happening this next week, and my best year would be absolutely ruined if all my plans got canceled. I better keep my lucky charm on me tight.

After we get home and put away the groceries, I head upstairs to my room to check on my lucky sea turtle. I open my pencil bag, and to my surprise, it's not there.

"Oh no," I whisper. Then I remind myself about the time I misplaced it at the Sea Musketeers meeting and take a deep breath.

I start searching around in my backpack, then in my bedroom. I begin to worry when I check under my bed and all I see are dust bunnies and a random shoe. I'm in full panic mode when I look in my sock drawer and all I find are socks!

Then I remember Jenny still has the second one that I lent her. Maybe I could convince Mom to go to her house before it starts snowing. I also think about how Chris and his dad say there is no such thing as bad or good luck. However, I can't believe that. Nearly everything was going great because of the sea turtle, and now it looks like everything is going terribly wrong. I take a breath and run downstairs.

I try to remain composed as I search for Mom. I find her standing silently by the window. She's watching the snow falling down.

"Good thing we went to the store when we did," she says.

I get a sinking feeling in my stomach as Mom motions for me to follow her.

"C'mon, let's do something fun to distract ourselves until we know how bad this storm really is."

I follow Mom, but as I walk away, I keep turning my head back toward the window. I don't think we're going anywhere right now. I've never felt so helpless.

Chapter Seventeen

I'm in the middle of doing a jigsaw puz-zle of sea animals with Mom when the cell phone beside her rings.

Mom takes a peek and nudges me. "It's Stanley."

I grab the phone and run up the stairs to my room. I hope Stanley has good news.

"Hi! Is the space party still on for tonight? What did your parents decide?"

He groans. "They said that we probably should cancel to be careful. Plus, it looks like we won't be able to see many meteors anyway. The skies are covered with clouds."

"I'm sorry, Stanley! That's such a bummer." I feel bad, so I do my best to cheer him up, like a good citizen would. "I'm sure everyone would love to still go whenever you reschedule your party."

He sighs. "Yeah, but this meteor shower only happens every so many years."

I pause and come up with a good idea.

"Maybe we can watch it online together. Plus, space is gigantic! It's a bazillion times bigger than the ocean. I'm sure there has to be something else amazing that we can see using your telescope."

"That's true," he says. I can tell he's still sad.

"Trust me. And thankfully that astronaut ice cream keeps forever."

Stanley laughs. "I feel a little better. Thanks, Stella!"

I begin to say "you're welcome" when suddenly, the lights go out. Thankfully, the sun hasn't set, so there is some light still coming through the windows.

"Stanley, is it dark at your place, too?"

"Whoa, it is. Hold on a second." I can hear Stanley mumbling to his parents. Then he says, "My dad wants me to get off the phone. I need to help him find the flashlights. I'll talk to you soon."

"Okay, bye."

I hang up the phone and head back downstairs.

"Mom? Nick?" I call out.

"*Estamos aquí, Stellita,*" Mom replies.

She walks toward me on the stairs and gives me a hug. "We better start a fire in the fireplace just in case the electricity stays off."

While she starts a fire, I check the window again. The weather has changed so quickly. In fact, it's almost a complete whiteout. There is so much snow, and the winds are strong.

Nick's phone buzzes. "There is an emergency alert. Winter storm warning," he reads aloud. "The Metra and all the buses are closed. They are telling everyone just to stay home."

I gulp. Then Mom's cell phone rings. "It's your *abuelos*; *espérame*." She walks away, telling us to wait.

"*Mande*," she answers.

I start to feel uneasy. Nick sees my worried expression.

"Hey, kiddo. Do you want to watch some Jacques Cousteau on my phone?"

I nod. He scoots over for me on the couch so I can sit beside him. Nick may be a moody older brother sometimes, but he's always there when I need him.

The video soothes me for a little while. The sounds of the ocean are almost like a lullaby. Mom walks back into the living room with a disappointed look on her face.

She sighs. "I'm so sorry to have to tell you, *niños* . . . your *abuelos'* flight got canceled. They are saying they can't reschedule it until a few days from now."

I feel my throat tighten, like it always does whenever I'm about to cry, but I hold it back.

Nick runs his fingers through his hair. "Hey, do you think we can video chat with them since they aren't coming?"

What a great idea! I give Nick a side hug, which makes him groan.

"I'm fragile," he says jokingly.

Mom smiles. "*Me encanta*, Nick. Let me see if Juanis can help. She canceled her trip to visit Maria to stay with them."

Mom grabs her phone to call. Nick and I begin to play thumb war when Mom abruptly stops.

I look over at Nick, who shrugs at me.

Mom frowns. "I hate to disappoint you two twice."

"What is it, Mom?" Nick asks.

"Our ceremony has officially been postponed from

Monday because of the weather. Don't worry, though. I am sure we will have the ceremony soon."

I throw my head in my hands. "And I bet we won't have the makeup meeting tomorrow for the Sea Musketeers. We really needed that rehearsal time."

I can feel Mom's hand on my arms. "It'll be okay. Your presentation isn't till Wednesday. There's still time."

"Okay," I reply as I lower my hands off my face. There are no tears. I couldn't cry even if I wanted to. I just feel angry. This is all happening because of the missing sea turtle.

Then I remember Linda. She has more of them in her closet at home. I have to get over there soon and get one before anything else goes wrong.

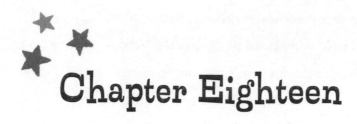

Chapter Eighteen

"Mom, we should go check on Linda," I say. "She's all by herself."

With extra sea turtles in her front hallway closet, I think.

Mom crosses her arms. "That's true. I've tried calling and texting her. She hasn't answered."

She walks over to the window. While there is at least two feet of snow, it's less of a whiteout. "It's slowed down some. It looks safe to walk just next door. Do you want to try walking with me?"

I nod.

Mom turns to Nick. "Will you be okay, *niño*?"

"Yeah, but be extra careful."

Mom and I put on as many layers as we can and

make sure that every inch of us is covered. That is, everything except for our eyeballs. When I take a peek in the mirror, it looks like we're going on a covert mission.

Mom says, "*¿Lista?*"

I clap my two heavy gloves together to signal that I'm ready.

Mom opens the door and a gust of wind comes in. While it's not subzero temperatures outside, the wind is strong and the snow is still falling. It means walking

takes much longer than usual. It feels similar to when you are wading in the waves on the beach.

After a few very long minutes, we eventually knock on Linda's door, and thankfully, she opens it right away.

She puts her hand on her chest. "Oh my goodness. Come in. Come in."

We are covered in snow and take off the wet outer layers in the mudroom. Biscuit is barking at first until he sees our faces. As soon as he recognizes us, he walks over to say hello.

Mom says, "We just wanted to check in on you. This all happened so quickly, we didn't know if you were prepared, and you weren't answering your phone."

"Thank you so much, darlings. I appreciate it." She hugs us both. "And yes, I was able to get to the store earlier. I've been getting weather updates on my favorite jazz radio station."

I pick up Biscuit and cradle him in my arms. Then I stare at Linda, wondering how I can ask her for a third sea turtle. Luckily, Mom's phone rings.

"It's Diego," she says, looking at her phone. She excuses herself into the next room. As I try to come up with the perfect words, I glance around Linda's place. It looks cozy. She has a few candles lit and an old radio playing classical jazz.

Linda looks at me. "Are you okay? You look like you have something to say."

I blurt out. "I lost my sea turtle, and I really need another one."

She frowns a little. "I'm sorry, Stella. I just gave the last one to my grandchild."

I can feel the disappointment fill my body. It's a mixture of anger and sadness again.

She raises her eyebrows. "Why did you need another one?"

I tap my foot and look down at the ground. I don't want to cry. I think Biscuit senses it because he licks my face a little bit. That relaxes me enough that I'm able to respond.

"Everything is going wrong since my sea turtle went missing. There is the snowstorm, my grandparents aren't coming, and our citizenship ceremony is postponed. This was going to be my year!"

I catch my breath and continue. "And I need to get my good luck back before anything else terrible happens, like the city council meeting gets canceled."

Linda lowers down to try to make eye contact with me. I keep staring at the ground.

"Stella, I promise with all my heart that none of this is happening because you lost a lucky charm."

I glance up for a second. That's a pretty big promise.

She continues. "Sometimes unexpected things happen that you can't control. While it's disappointing, you just have to roll with it. And the wonderful things happening in your life are because you and your mama worked hard for them. Not a sea turtle figurine. No one is taking those accomplishments away from you."

I raise my head and look at her. She's kind of making sense, and her face looks sincere.

She adds, "I got you the sea turtle mostly because you love the oceans. Plus, I had a lucky rabbit's foot growing up, and it made me feel happy every time I saw it. I was hoping that the turtle would do the same for you."

I smile at her. "It did make me happy."

Then I think about what she said. "A real rabbit's foot?"

She laughs.

"It's weird. I know. I don't know if they even sell those anymore."

Suddenly, the lights turn back on. The beeping of different electronics causes Biscuit to wiggle out of my arms. I put him back on the ground so he can go inspect as Mom walks back into the room.

She looks at the ceiling and exclaims, "¡Gracias!"

"How's Diego?" Linda asks, standing back up.

"He's fine; he just wanted to see if we were okay," she says as she puts her phone in her pocket. "We should go back home to your brother in case the storm picks up."

I look up at Linda. While it looks cozy here, I don't want her to be by herself during the storm.

"Do you and Biscuit want to join us next door?"

Mom chimes in. "Yes, please come over. We've got plenty of food, and we've got the fireplace going."

Linda nods. "That's an offer I can't refuse."

We make sure to bundle them both up. Linda also puts together an overnight bag for her and Biscuit. Mom carries the bag because Linda's busy carrying Biscuit. She tucks him inside her jacket so he will stay warm and protected from the elements. It's such a cute sight to see his little head in his parka poking out of the top of Linda's jacket. Thankfully, the wind has slowed down, but it seems like the snow is even taller. It's almost as tall as my hips. At least we have a trail in the snow from when we walked over.

When we make it back inside, Nick hops over on his crutches to greet us at the door.

"I was just about to hobble over there and save you."

I hug him and almost knock him over. While he can be a grump, he does love us.

Mom goes to make Abuelita hot chocolate in the kitchen. Linda unzips her jacket and lets Biscuit down onto the ground.

She sits on the couch next to Nick and tells him, "Trust me, you should be happy to be sitting. That was a very tiring walk."

She pulls her crochet from her overnight bag. Biscuit in the meantime lowers down onto his front two paws in puppy position. This means he is ready to play. Linda hands me a toy, and I toss it toward him. He prances to pick it up, and then he runs around the room with his squeaky toy in his mouth. As I chase after him, my sadness fades away and is replaced with another feeling. While I'm disappointed about the storm, at least we get to spend some more time with Linda and Biscuit.

Then I remember Nick's great idea. I run up to Mom.

"Could we still video chat with Apolinar and Maria?"

Nick sits up. "Yeah, it would be fun to see them."

Mom nods. "Let me check. Juanis should be able to set that up."

Mom grabs the laptop and her phone. Luckily, they are at home just playing canasta and are able to chat.

With a little work on both ends, they finally show up on the computer screen. It warms my heart to see them sitting there.

"*Hola, mis amores. ¿Cómo están?*" They greet us and ask how we are.

I jump in before anyone else can speak. This is my chance to show them how much I have been practicing.

"*Estamos bien, pero estoy triste que no voy a verte mañana.*" I reply that we're good, but that I am sad that I'm not going to see them tomorrow.

Mom throws her arm around my shoulder. From her expression, I can tell she's proud.

"*¡Stella, suenas bien! ¡Que maravilloso!*" They respond that it's marvelous, that I sound great.

I grin. It would have been nice to hear that in person, but this is not bad.

"*¡Voy a practicar mas!*" I reply that I'm going to practice more.

Mom starts talking to them about the weather and how we are okay. Nick shows them his cast. They promise they will still come to visit, but that they might wait till May, when the weather is warmer.

Apolinar says, "*Pero no te preocupes. Vamos a festejar en mayo. Estamos orgulloso de ustedes.*"

It makes me happy to hear we're still going to celebrate in May and especially that they are proud of us.

After we leave the chat, I say to Mom, "Could I do another video chat during the blizzard?"

Mom raises an eyebrow. "With whom?"

"I'm thinking we could have a Sea Musketeers meeting tomorrow."

Mom side hugs me. "You two are full of great ideas."

I reply, "Sometimes."

The rest of the night, we play cards and watch animated movies. Mom even makes *sopa de tortilla* to warm our bellies. Tortilla soup is especially helpful after you have to take Biscuit into the backyard for the world's fastest bathroom break.

I look around the room. While there is some disappointment that things didn't go according to plan, I am just happy to be with my family and friends.

Chapter Nineteen

Monday and Tuesday, we are still stuck at home. At first, we try to make the blizzard as fun as possible. For instance, on Monday, we have a pancake buffet and a Lord of the Rings movie marathon, although I spend most of the movies working on my portrait of Ms. Benedetto.

On Tuesday, the fun energy deflates to zero. Nick stays busy by playing video games, Mom works from home, and I video chat with the Sea Musketeers to rehearse. I also work on memorizing my lines for the presentation. Then I quickly run out of things to do. Being stuck at home can feel annoying, but the experience makes me realize why Nick has been so grumpy. It wasn't that I wasn't helpful enough. It was just annoying for Nick to be in the same spot with fewer options of things to do. Mom had tried to explain that to me, but I hadn't wanted to listen.

By Wednesday morning, we are all enthusiastic to leave the house and return to normal, especially Nick. He's humming to himself as he throws on his backpack. He even begins to sing off-key. "Oh, it's the last day with my cast! How I can't wait till tomorrow!"

I chuckle. "Will you keep the cast?"

He sticks out his leg. "Of course! I can't lose this beauty."

We both carefully examine it. There are so many signatures that you can't make out some of the names at all. That is, except for the place where I drew my octopus. Nick made sure to keep that preserved.

I grin to myself, but I don't mention it to him. Instead I say, "Well, I can't wait till tonight."

This evening is the Sea Musketeers presentation in front of the city council. Even though we have rehearsed it so many times, I am still pretty nervous.

He messes with my curls. "You're going to do great."

When I arrive at school, I walk carefully as I carry my portrait of Ms. Benedetto in my hands. I spy Chris holding his portfolio case as he walks up to the building. I nervously wave, and, to my surprise, he waves me over.

I ask, "Is that your portrait of Ms. Benedetto?"

He nods.

There is a giant pause, and then I just let it all out.

"I'm really sorry, Chris. I just got obsessed with wanting to fix everything, and then I was convinced my sea turtle could really help. I realized during the snowstorm how silly that all was."

He nods. "I understand. I was sensitive, too. It's just that it's happened before. People always think my dad is helpless, but he can still do so much. I just want us to be treated like we're a normal family, because we are."

I frown. I never considered how hard that must be. To always have that sort of pressure on you.

I say, "I am starting to understand that."

"I know, Stella," he says. "You're a good person."

I sigh, feeling relieved. "And I promise not to bring

it up unless you want to talk about it. Although I do want to say, your dad is pretty cool."

"Duh," he replies with a smile. "He's always been cool."

We resume walking. "Do you think Ms. Benedetto is going to freak out when she sees our portraits?"

"Completely."

And he was right. Ms. Benedetto practically bawls when she sees almost two dozen portraits of herself from all the club members.

"Thank you!" she says, rubbing her eyes.

Later that night, before the city council presentation, the Sea Musketeers meet for deep-dish pizza and one last rehearsal, and to discuss our plan with Mr. Kyle. We show him our slideshow for a final check. He scrolls at the laptop while the rest of us keep our messy hands away.

"I'm so impressed with all the work you've done," Mr. Kyle says.

"Do you think we have a chance to get it passed?" I ask in between bites.

He nods.

"I also let my friend know about your presentation," he says. "She's a journalist, so she's going to come and perhaps write an article about this. The more exposure we can get, the better it will help your cause."

I squeal, but then my stomach immediately turns a bit. I suddenly lose my appetite. I open and close for the group's presentation. I really have to nail it. This is so much pressure.

When we arrive at city hall, we have to wait outside before it's our turn. I take a peek through the crack of the door. I can see the board is sitting up on a high platform. They look stern, like judges. I feel my legs shaking a bit with each step back to my group. I don't think I can do this. I'm searching my backpack for my note cards when I spy something familiar in the very bottom of the bag. I pull it out slowly. It's my lucky sea turtle, and it's been there this entire time! Then I remember my conversation with Linda, and it makes me smile. I take a deep breath.

A man with a clipboard opens the door. He looks confused as he says, "The . . . Sea Musketeers?"

"That's us," Logan says.

The man looks at us. "Are you all ready?"

I reply, "Yes, we are."

Stanley and Jenny then link arms with me, and we head in for the presentation.

Chapter Twenty

"How do I look?" Nick says.

He's coming down the stairs in a button-up shirt and dress pants.

"*Muy guapo*," Mom says, giving him a kiss on the cheek.

He groans, but he doesn't wipe it off his face.

"You look like a future citizen," I say, tugging at my new sweater. It's navy blue and white and matches well with my red skirt.

"I'll always be an alien in my heart." He raises two fingers above his head like alien antennas.

It's the end of March. Thankfully, we were able to

reschedule our citizenship ceremony for just a couple of weeks later. Nick is also back to work at the pizza shop. The biggest news is that the city council approved our plastics pledge. All the schools will work to reduce plastic consumption by 50 percent. Mr. Kyle's journalist friend is also going to write an article about the Sea Musketeers and our crusade. We are going to meet with her soon so she can ask us questions and learn more about us. Best of all, Maria and Apolinar rescheduled their flights for the end of May. With such exciting plans on the horizon, I realize that the year isn't over yet. It's only March! Who knows? It could still be the best one ever.

Mom checks her purse as we walk toward the front door.

"I've got our IDs and everything for the ceremony. *Vamos, niños*."

Our ceremony is early in the morning, which means we have to miss a little bit of school and work to attend. Then later tonight, we are going to have our big celebration—a party at our house. When we step outside, I notice that a small tree on our block has little white blossoms.

"It looks like spring is coming," I say.

"You never know with Chicago weather," Nick replies with a wink.

We park our car at the local Metra stop and ride the train downtown. Mom usually takes the Metra to work during the week. We are all grins as we ride on the crowded train. As much as I wish I could shout to the other riders where we are going, everyone looks too busy. But then I get my chance.

An older man says, "Don't you all look fancy."

"We're going to our citizenship ceremony!" I reply proudly.

"Congrats!" He flashes us a thumbs-up.

When we arrive at our stop, we walk a few blocks to a large government building. As we enter, we have to walk through metal detectors. It makes me feel like we're on a top secret mission.

The building is huge, but luckily, we are directed

to the right room. After we walk through the double doors, Mom speaks with a stern-looking official behind plexiglass.

"Identification?" she asks us.

Mom passes it to her through the window. "We're the Díaz family. I'm Perla, and I have my two kids with me, Nicolas and Estrella."

The official types on a computer. Then she flips through some folders and pulls out our citizenship certificates. She hands them to us.

"Please sign on your photograph along the left side and take a seat."

"Thank you!" I reply, and she flashes a smile back at me.

We head over to the chairs lined up for the assembly and take a seat. After I sign my full name, I stare at this sheet of paper. It says *The United States of America* in big letters across the top. There is even my age, my height, and small cursive script. On the bottom left is a little picture of me. We took this picture a few months ago. Even though I'm not smiling in the photograph,

I can see how proud I felt in that moment. Just like right now. I look over at Mom. She stares down at her own certificate.

"We did it, Mom." I nudge her with my elbow.

She nods. I can see her eyes welling up with tears.

Nick throws his arm around her shoulder. "*You* did it, Mom."

Mom looks up at the ceiling. "*Niños*, you're going to make me cry. I don't want pictures of my mascara running."

She shakes off the tears and then poses Nick and me together for a photo. Then she asks a man to take a picture of the three of us. She returns the favor and takes a picture of him as well.

As I look across the room, I see so many people from different places. But what unites us all is the excitement for this moment. The moment that many of us thought might never come. I tap my foot with anticipation as I read my citizenship oath. I've read it to myself a few times, so I should be ready.

Finally a judge comes in and has us all stand up to say our oath of allegiance. It's just like Mr. Don described! We have to place our hands over our hearts while we say it. There are a few words I have a hard time pronouncing during the ceremony, so I just mumble them. I should have practiced it aloud!

Once the ceremony has finished, we all applaud. Mom takes our certificates and places them carefully back into their special envelopes before storing them in her briefcase. That's when I realize something. Now that we are officially citizens, I have completed two of my resolutions. It's only March, too. Maybe I need to come up with a few new ones!

On the way back to the Metra, I ask Mom and Nick to explain some of those tricky words to me. I pull out the oath and point to the word that was the hardest for me to say.

"What does *renoose* mean?"

"You mean *renounce*," says Nick. "It means to give up."

"Oh . . . ," I reply. "Give up being Mexican." That's a little tough to swallow.

Nick turns toward me. "I've been thinking about it a lot. No one can take your identity from you. We're always Mexican, just like we're also aliens at heart. It's just now we're officially citizens, too."

I smile. I love that I can be so many things at once.

A girl.

A Mexican.

An American.

An artist.

And a Sea Musketeer.

That's pretty special. Sea turtle or no sea turtle, I'm pretty lucky.

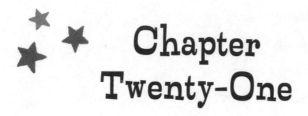

Chapter
Twenty-One

I look around the house. I thought we
had a lot of people over at New Year's, but this is the
most people that we've ever had inside our house at
once. While this isn't as large as the party we had at
school for Mr. Don, there is still a very large cake.

Linda helped us bake it. We decided to do half
vanilla and half chocolate since it was hard to choose
just one flavor. We even decorated it on top with blueberries and strawberries to make it look like an American flag.

Around the living room, I spy Stanley, Jenny, the rest
of the Sea Musketeers, Diego, Izzy, Linda, Biscuit, and

even Chris with his parents. Nick invited a few people, like Erika and Jason. All to celebrate our big day.

I walk over to Nick and his group and whisper, "Is Erika your girlfriend?"

He turns *rojo* and then whispers, "Maybe," just as Erika turns to me and asks, "How do you feel now that you are a US citizen?"

I think about it, and I come up with the perfect answer. "As happy as a puffer fish."

Erika looks confused.

I explain. "I saw a picture once, and they are so cute! They look like they're smiling."

"Oh." She scratches her head.

Jason pulls up a picture on his phone and shows her.

Erika replies, "Ohhhhhh! It does look happy!"

Nick flashes the alien antennas to me. I smile. Nick's gesture reminds me of a great idea I had. I walk over to Mom, who is talking to Diego and Linda.

"*Sí, mi Stellita,*" says Mom.

"I've been thinking. Do you think we could maybe frame our Mexican passports?"

She clasps her hands together. "That's a sweet idea. It would be a good way to treasure them."

Biscuit then runs up to me, and I lift him into the air. He licks my face, which makes me giggle.

Mom rests her hand against her cheek. "You really love that dog, don't you?"

I smoosh him against me. "Absolutely."

She pats Biscuit on the head. "I think it's maybe time we get you your own dog for your birthday."

"Really?!" I squeal.

She hugs me. "You've proved to me that you are a great dog caregiver, and you'll be ten years old, too. I think that is old enough to handle that responsibility."

"¡Gracias!" I am so happy!

Linda winks at me as I lower Biscuit back onto the ground. I run over to my friends and share my good news about the dog.

Chris gives me a high five. "That's awesome! I love dogs, especially my dad's dog, Summer."

"Do you have to walk her for your dad?" I ask curiously.

Chris shakes his head. "He walks her most of the time."

I turn *roja*.

Then he adds with a sympathetic smile, "But they had to train how to walk together."

I nod. There is so much I'm still learning, and I'm glad Chris understands that.

Then Jenny says, "Oh, let's come up with a list of dog names."

Stanley grabs a pencil and a sheet of paper. "I'll keep a list of all the names."

Logan says, "What about the name Waffles?"

Kristen shakes her head. "No. It should be Bella. It is cute, plus it rhymes with Stella."

"That's true, but I like both." I scratch my chin. "I guess we should come up with names for a boy or girl dog."

Mariel elbows me. *"Buena idea."*

We spend the rest of the party eating cake and coming up with names.

For a moment, I remember when I thought everything was ending and ruined. When I look around me, though, I realize it's like sailing across an ocean. Sometimes a big wave or storm throws everything off track, but once you pop up again, things eventually get back to normal. I may not know what's ahead, but with my trusty crew of people, I think I'll weather it very well.

Author's Note

As with all my books with Stella Díaz, I drew from my own personal experiences. For example, I also became a United States citizen after living in the US for a while. Unlike Stella, though, that didn't happen for me until I was twenty-one years old. It also worked out that I ended up having the ceremony all by myself a few months after my mom and brother. However, this is one of the reasons why writing is magical to me. Through this story, I was able to create the way I wish my ceremony would have gone and give it to Stella. Regardless of how it happened, I can still remember all the excitement and nervousness I felt. It's a ceremony that not everyone gets to experience, but if they do, it definitely imprints on them. Like Stella, to this day, I'm proud to not only be a citizen but also an immigrant.

Here I am with my brother, mother, abuelos, and tía in Mexico City.

But probably one of my biggest inspirations for writing this book was the challenging year that was 2020. It was the year that many plans had to be rescheduled or just flat-out canceled. At any age, that can be tough. However, I appreciate that I was fortunate enough to take all those emotions and channel them into this story. It's a story I hope you all will love and relate to.

Finally, my last big inspiration came from my real-life friend and loudest kid in the classroom, Chris Pollard. I have to thank him for allowing me to share his family's experience with PLS. Seeing how their family came together in recent years has been an amazing sight. Thank you, Chris, for always being my friend and for the "Van Go" joke.

Acknowledgments

Thank you, dear reader, for reading another Stella Díaz. Can you believe it's the fourth book? Whew! I have to thank my beta readers: Mary, Kyle, and Mom. I'd also like to thank my petite dog, Petunia. Thank for you cuddling on my lap while I worked. (And yes, I do think Petunia and Biscuit would be best buds.)

I'd also like to thank the people involved in the creation of this book. Thank you to my agent, Linda Pratt, and my great editorial team, Connie Hsu and Megan Abbate. Connie and Megan, you push me every time, and I'm a better author because of you. A huge thank-you to Kristie Radwilowicz and Elizabeth Holden Clark for their wonderful work on the design of the book. Thank you to everyone at Roaring Brook and Macmillan Children's, including Jennifer Besser, Allison Verost, Jen Edwards, Avia Perez, John Nora, Jordin Streeter, and Nico Ore-Giron. I have to also thank the marketing and publicity teams at Macmillan, especially Mary Van Akin and Cynthia Lliguichuzhca. Thank you for championing this book and getting it into the hands of educators and librarians. You are the best!

And finally, to everyone who has read Stella. I started working on the first concept in 2013, and look where it is now! A . . . M . . . A . . . Z . . . I . . . N . . . G. I hope that you, dear readers, always "have something to say," that you "never give up," and most importantly, that you "dream big."

Resources

1. To learn more about how your school can reduce waste, please visit: pca.state.mn.us/creating-less -trash-school
2. To learn more information about people with disabilities, please visit:
   American Association of People with Disabilities
   aapd.com
3. To learn more information on primary lateral sclerosis:
   National Organization of Rare Disorders
   rarediseases.org/rare-diseases/primary-lateral -sclerosis
4. To learn more about the Art Institute of Chicago: artic.edu

DON'T MISS THE OTHER BOOKS STARRING STELLA DÍAZ!